# CROSSING
## *The* LINE

### ZOEY LOCKE
### Z.L. ARKADIE

# A Happy Accident

PAISLEY GROVE

"It's you." Those words escape past my lips in a whisper.

I'm trapped in his gaze. I can hardly believe I'm looking at Hercules Lord. His eyes haven't changed at all since I last saw him. They still have the sort of depth that's able to see straight into my soul—and they are very, very, *very* seductive.

*How long has it been? Seven, eight years? Something in between?* The last time we gaped at each other this way comes back in a rushed memory. We were in Boston. First, we were at a New Year's Eve party, and then we went to his place.

"PG," Hercules says, savoring each letter.

My face is suddenly flushed with warmth as I'm only barely able to say, "Hi." I clear my throat, determined to sound less flustered the next time I speak.

"Hello. What a…" His words hang in the air, gently wafting over me for a few moments. "Pleasant surprise."

"So, the two of you know each other?" my new friend Lake Carlton asks. I almost forgot that Hercules and I aren't alone.

It's hard to rip my concentration away from his extraordinarily handsome face. Trimmed stubble layer his dimpled chin and sharp jawline. His dark eyebrows are neat, teeth white and he still has good skin. And a delicious freshly laundered scent rises from his tailored shirt. From high school to college to now, age has been so good to him.

I'm finally able to focus on Lake, who looks quite stunning tonight. She's wearing a silky white halter dress that displays her bare shoulders, which appear as supple as soft cotton balls under the warm lights of the chic venue. And her dark chin-length wavy hair complements her graceful swan's neck.

I arrived at Lake and "Kirkie's" engagement party moments ago, and when I finally located her, she was conversing with a tall, well-built Adonis of a man. At first, I admired the guy from behind, planning to wait until their conversation ended before approaching. But something about him led me to close the distance between us right then and there. Then I saw his face. My instincts had served me well. I did know the sexy stranger with the alluring rear view. I knew him very well.

Something suddenly dawns on me, and I slap a hand over my rapidly beating heart. "Wait. Is Hercules *Kirkie*?" I ask Lake.

Hercules crunches his eyebrows. "What's a Kirkie?"

*Gosh, he's so beautiful when he makes that face.*

"No, no, no," Lake says, shaking her head with each denial. She puts her long fingers on Hercules's fit bicep. "Mason is Kirkie."

Hercules's confused expression intensifies. "Mason is Kirkie?"

Lake presses a hand next to her mouth as if she's about to tell him a secret. "It's what I call him when he's not around."

"Ah…" Hercules says, laughing as his head tips back.

I can barely focus on Lake when she tells me that Hercules is Mason's—Kirkie's—best man, best friend, and boss. One thing's for certain: I dodged a bullet. I wouldn't know what to do or how to feel if

Lake introduced the man I've always had an epic crush on as her fiancé. I probably would've fainted or something.

"So really, how do the two of you know each other?" Lake's pointed finger shifts between Hercules and me like a windshield wiper.

"High school," we say at the same time.

I beam at him and he at me. My face is warm and has probably turned a dusty rose by now. I'm embarrassed about that. I want to appear like someone who doesn't go all schoolgirl crush in the presence of the man she's never been able to get out of her system. I'm darn near thirty. I should be better at interacting with him by now.

Wearing my best, most confident smile, I add, "Well, we met in high school, but we last saw each other my final year in college."

Hercules winks at me. "Yes. That's our story."

Lake's slow smile builds as she watches us as though Hercules and I are rare creatures that she must learn absolutely everything about. "Then you have a story?"

"What?" I croak. My head is spinning.

"You have a story. Does that mean the two of you were involved at some point?"

Hercules folds his hard arms high on his broad chest. "Clarify 'involved'?"

Tapering an eye suspiciously, Lake says, "You fully know good and well what I mean by 'involved,' Hercules. Stop stalling."

Hercules flashes his trademark sexy, lopsided grin, one that I remember so well. "We're old friends, Lake."

Lake posts her amused expression on me as though she's seeking corroboration. I'm so lost for words and too flustered to respond to the look on her face.

The truth is, we weren't always friends. We were both students at Dorset Meacham Academy, a private high school on the Upper East Side. Before the start of my senior year, I still lived in California, but after my grandfather died, my mom and dad relocated to Manhattan, and I had to go with them. And although I had nearly worshipped Hercules from the moment I laid eyes on him, we didn't really say more than "hi" or "thanks" to each other until one fateful Monday afternoon when he showed up late to our fifth-period computer-programming class.

Minutes before he arrived, Mr. Northam had asked us to pair up for the next assignment. As usual, I ended up without a partner even though my classmates knew teaming up with me was a guaranteed A-plus. The entire school knew I was a computer-coding genius. While Mr. Northam pondered which duo needed a third person, Hercules gusted into the classroom and plopped down in his regular seat.

"Aha, you two," Mr. Northam said, peering at us over the top of his horn-rimmed glasses. "Problem solved."

But the problem wasn't solved. Everyone knew that our families, the Lords and the Groves, were enemies. As a matter of fact, I'd heard plenty enough times that Dorset Meacham Academy— DMA—was Lord country. Even though Hercules and I never showed any overt disdain for each other, the rule was set long before he or I arrived. Before us, his brother Orion and my cousin Lynx had fought tirelessly to dominate DMA's hallowed halls and win social dominance for one family and ruin for the other. Orion had been the victor, leaving Lynx—and then me—hopelessly trying to figure out how to survive DMA's jagged, Lord-polluted terrain.

Lake is still waiting for me to confirm Hercules's claim.

"Yes, we are old friends, I say to keep the explanation of our complicated history simple.

He and I stare at each other with conspiratorial grins.

Lake starts to say something but thankfully Hercules quickly turns to her and says, "But wait a minute. Does Mason know you call him as Kirkie when he's not looking?"

"Oh no, you called me that name in public, babe?" A tall, dark, and very handsome man slips into our circle of three, positioning himself between Hercules and Lake. Once he's in place, he curls an arm around Lake's narrow waist.

Lake giggles as she kisses her fiancé and then asks where has he been. She and Mason are a striking couple. He has a charming quality. And ever since we met, she's proven to me that she just might be the happiest woman on earth. She's always smiling, content, and looking on the bright side of stressful situations.

"Your cousin's a pill," he says, complaining wearily.

Lake's grunt expresses that she understands his tone.

But I'm back to gazing into Hercules's eyes as Lake introduces me to her fiancé. My chest rises high as I inhale deeply and then retracts with deliberate control as I release my breath. I'll admit that, momentarily, I am completely under Hercules Lord's spell.

"Whoa, is she—are you—*the* Paisley Grove?" Mason asks.

I'm on the verge of turning to get a look at the expression behind the way Mason asked that question, but I'm unable to take my eyes off the gorgeous woman who links arms with the man of my dreams. She's wearing a silver body-con dress that's so short and with a neckline so deep that it leaves nothing to the imagination.

She holds Hercules tighter. That one possessive act makes me focus on how Hercules's crisp black shirt clings to his perfect, not overly muscular but very strong bicep. I also notice how delicate her feminine arms appear next to his.

When my gaze finds its way to her face, her eyes are grinning deviously at me, but her lips are not. That's when realization slams into me like a tsunami. *Holy moly—this woman has just come out of nowhere to claim the man of my dreams.*

# The Party Must Go On

PAISLEY GROVE

"Here you are," the model-like woman croons in a high-pitched, sultry voice that sounds practiced.

She's definitely a sight for sore eyes—I'll admit that. I'll also admit that her presence makes me feel inadequate. I grace her with a welcoming smile. She doesn't smile back though. Her eyes merely pass over me as though I'm of no concern to her. She's not friendly I see. It's sort of disappointing that Hercules would choose such an ice queen. Maybe I don't know him as well as I thought I did. The version of Hercules that I had desired for far longer than I should've is way too discerning to be with a stuck-up person like Lauren.

"Then you *are* Paisley Grove, Max Grove's sister?" Mason asks again.

When I look at Mason, it's as if I'm seeing right through him. I'm very not present for this moment. I feel as if I'm being rude. Or maybe it's he who is being rude. I can't make that determination at the moment. I'm too out of sorts.

"Yes, I am," I say.

Mason tosses a stunned look at Lake and then at Hercules. I'm sure he knows all about our family feud since he's Hercules's best friend. It seems like he's not happy to meet me or see me at his party. My insides cringe. I haven't felt this uncomfortable since stepping onto the grounds of Lord country back in high school.

"You have a great turnout for a Thursday night," Hercules's date says to Lake, who passes a glance around the room as she agrees.

I turn to locate the hallway that leads to the elevators. I should leave soon.

"Oh, by the way, Lauren," Lake says, gripping my forearm as if she can sense that I want to escape her party. "This is my *friend* Paisley." Lake raises her eyebrows at Mason as if she's warning him to be nice to me.

Lauren presses her overly red lips together and

grunts dismissively as she clings tighter to Hercules. That is her not-so-subtle way of letting me know that she's not going to shake hands.

Hercules folds his arms over his broad chest, effortlessly freeing himself from Lauren's strait-jacket-like hold. "So, how did the two of you become friends?" he says as his amused gaze bounces between Lake and me.

Lake recounts the moment that we became fast besties. She was my last interview of the day. I was hiring an artist to design all the signage and branding for our company's annual Endow the World with Technology benefit. All morning, Max, my older brother and CEO of GIT—Grove Industrial Technologies—a title he shares with my uncle, Leo Grove, had been riding me for one reason or another. He hates that I'm working in PR and not product development. That's why he consistently makes my job hard, always sending me emails about what I've done wrong, what I missed, and what—as the public relations director—I should know. It was because of his badgering that I could hardly focus during Lake's interview.

Then she abruptly stood and said, "I've got a feeling you need to get the hell out of this office. Am I right?"

I looked at her, shocked that she had done something that was so unusual. I thought she was bold. My default reply would've been to say that I was fine. But I wasn't fine. The walls of my office felt as though they had been caving in on me all morning. So, instead of smiling politely and then getting on with the interview, I nodded.

"Okay, then," she said, pointing her head toward the way out. "Let's make a break for it."

We walked and talked and shopped. Lake led me into stores that I never knew existed. I bought trinkets. We perused galleries for artwork, where she showed me some of her pieces. I even bought two oil paintings of hers, abstracts that I found emotionally moving. One is hanging in my office. Max was enthralled by the other painting, so I gave it to him. The time we spent together went by so fast. When we parted, I told her she had the job, and we exchanged phone numbers. Since then, every day that we're not working together, we're on the phone talking to each other.

"Our conversations are endless, don't you think?" she asks me.

My smile is large and happy. "I think so."

The way Hercules grins at me makes me blush. It's as if Lake and my strong connection moves him.

"I even know her favorite color," Lake says.

I chuckle because Lake's on a roll, being her charming self. "And I know yours."

She says "Black" at the same time that I say "Yellow."

Hercules's appraising eyes dip down and rise back up my body. "I would've guessed red," he whispers.

I quickly look down at my cousin Treasure's formfitting and fairly sexy red cocktail dress that I'm wearing. *Should I admit that it doesn't belong to me?*

Hercules's lips part as if he's about to say something else, but a bossy voice comes over the loudspeaker, demanding that the happy couple come to the front immediately, *right now*.

"That's my cousin, Amy," Lake says in my ear and rolls her eyes. "I've been forced to make her my maid of honor."

Lake raises her eyebrows at Mason, and they walk off together, heading toward the big windows where a microphone stand is set up. As they split the crowd, people clap.

I'm hiding my panic, realizing Lake and Mason have left me alone with Hercules and Lauren. I close my eyes for a few seconds, bracing myself, before turning to face them. And right on cue,

Lauren wraps herself around Hercules's arm yet again, showing me that he belongs to her.

I'm trying to smile, but I don't succeed. "Excuse me," I say, and as fast as my feet will carry me without running, I move away from the happy couple. Or maybe they aren't so happy. I can't figure it out.

The faster I walk away from them, though, the more relieved I feel. I glance over each shoulder and then sigh with relief. *Good job, Pais. You have allowed yourself to become lost in the crowd.*

I must force myself to forget that Hercules is here tonight. *He has a date, Paisley.* If I can remember that, repeat it until it sinks in, then he will have no power over me.

———

About two hours later, the festivities are in full swing. Cocktails are flowing from the free bar, and jovial conversations bounce around the room like a volleyball. One thing's for sure—New Yorkers sure do know how to party. After Mason and Lake made speeches declaring their love for each other, the music began. The couple of honor started dancing, and more and more people joined them on the wooden dance floor that had been set up in front of the enormous picture windows.

Watching bodies dance with the lit city in the background has an artistic appeal. I'm certain Lake arranged the scene that way on purpose. It's such an artistic thing to do.

I've plopped myself on a stool at one of the high, round tables lining the perimeter of the venue. I'm still trying to stay away from Hercules. I don't want to even catch a glance of him and Lauren together. The sight of them standing close while she whispers sweet nothings in his ear doesn't make me feel so swell.

Every now and then, a guy takes a seat next to me and asks if I want to dance. I graciously decline. It's not that I don't want to get in the mix and have a good time. I just don't want to be seen. I'm hiding.

So far, Hercules and Lauren haven't hit the dance floor. But I must admit it would be nice to see if Hercules has any good moves. I bet he's a sexy dancer. It's the way he walks and all his gestures—he's masculine but graceful. *Very sensuous.*

In my mind's eye, I've been analyzing his body language with Lauren. *When she clung to his arm earlier, did he look uncomfortable?* I'm not sure, though. He didn't try to take his arm back from her. If he was into me at all, then he would've found a way to free himself from her. I think he was just being nice to me before Lauren showed up. Just like in high school.

"Hey." Lake hops up onto the stool beside me.

I jump because I didn't see her coming. "Hey."

Lake curls an arm around my waist. "Get up, sexy lady in red. You're going to dance." Her tone is singsong, eyes gleam with excitement and she's so buzzed. I'm pretty sure she's had a cocktail or two or three.

"I don't dance," I shout over a peppy song.

"Everybody dances, Paisley!"

After more coaxing, I reluctantly slide off my stool and allow Lake to guide me to the dance floor. After all, it's her party, and it would be rude to say no to a twirl with the future bride.

When we mark our spot among the other dancing bodies, Lake rolls her arms above her head as she curls her hips toward the floor. Her moves are smooth and graceful. With a raised eyebrow, she encourages me to follow her lead.

My face is warm as I look around nervously. People are watching me. A lot of them are men. I think it's because of Treasure's red dress. I should never have worn it. By Treasure's standards, the garment is doing its job. She likes to be seen. I, on the other hand, do not. The attention makes me nervous.

"Come on, Pais. You can do it. Let loose!" Lake says before circling her arms above her head and twirling.

I release a deep sigh as I shuffle halfheartedly from side to side. It's not that I can't dance. I can dance. In junior high, modern dance was one of my extracurricular activities, and I was good at it. The only reason I stopped was because my parents thought that in high school, I should focus more on what was viable for my future—computer programming.

I pull from my memory bank and start swaying my hips and twirling my arms.

"That's it!" Lake exclaims, clapping excitedly.

Still moving my hips, I blush, embarrassed, into the palm of my hand. I must admit, dancing like this feels so good, so freeing. That's probably the main reason I've been so drawn to Lake as a friend. She knows how to coax me into doing things I would've never done on my own. Kind of like my cousin, Treasure, who has been my best friend since she first taught me how to annoy parents by endlessly shaking my rattle.

"What were you talking about?" Lake grabs both my hands as we twist our hips like a corkscrew toward the floor together. "You're a fantastic dancer," she exclaims.

"I never said I couldn't dance. I said I don't dance," I shout above the music.

Her head falls back as she laughs. Then she draws me nearer and, with her mouth close to my ear, says, "And oh my God, Hercules has a thing for you."

When she pulls back to see my face, I'm confused. "But he has a girlfriend," I say loudly enough for her to hear over the music but not loud enough to be heard by anyone else.

"Girlfriend?" She screws her face. "It's complicated."

"Then she's not his girlfriend?"

Lake's eyebrows furrow and then even out. I can tell she's holding back from telling me the whole story. Then she pulls me close again. "Hercules is hot as sin and rich as hell, and I've never seen him show that much interest in any woman since you came along. And that includes Lauren. I'm mean, look at him over there. He can't take his eyes off of you."

I don't see Hercules at all. "Over where?"

"Directly over your right shoulder," Lake says.

I whip my face around probably a little too fast. And in an instant, my searching eyes connect with his.

# Who's That Guy?

PAISLEY GROVE

No, Hercules isn't watching me. He's leering at me while Lauren stands next to him with her lips near his ear. It doesn't look as if he's paying attention to whatever she's saying. He's zeroed in on me.

My body responds to our eye contact as I succumb to the sexual trance that his staring puts me in. I'm combing my fingers through my hair as I swivel my hips seductively, picturing myself on Hercules's cock as my teeth seize my bottom lip. That's when I realize that he's chewing on his lip too. I should look away from him, but I can't. I should release my lower lip, but I can't do that either. It's something I do when I'm turned on. His stare turns me on.

When Lauren slaps him on the shoulder, it's as if she's nudging me out of my lustful daze too. Inhaling sharply, I turn away from the couple. *What just happened? And what does Lake mean by their relationship being complicated?*

I want to implore Lake to please tell me everything she knows about Hercules and Lauren, but her serious cousin Amy—who's definitely not having as much fun as the rest of us—is whispering in her ear. After rolling her eyes, Lake spins away from me and follows Amy away from the dance floor. I'm starting to think that Lake and her cousin aren't cut from the same cloth.

I find that I prefer dancing to sitting, since the exercise gives me something to do. Fortunately, a guy slides over to dance with me. Shifting my feet from side to side, I tilt my head, recognizing him as the guy who sat next to me at the table when I chose to be a wallflower.

He leans in, guiding his mouth toward my ear. I incline forward to hear him.

"So, you do dance," he says.

I toss my head back and laugh. I'm tempted to search for Hercules to see how his conversation with Lauren is progressing, but I keep my attention glued to my new dance partner's face. He's cute. If Hercules wasn't in the vicinity, I would be thrilled that this sexy stranger had chosen to pursue me.

The guy bends toward me again, and his warm minty breath drifts across my face when he says, "I'm Clive."

I move closer so he can hear me over the music. "I'm Paisley." Not only does Clive's breath smell delicious, but so does the rest of him. His cologne is citrusy with hints of sandalwood and vanilla.

Inclining my ear more toward Clive to hear him better as he tells me how good of a dancer I am, I catch a glimpse of Hercules. Arms crossed and stance wide, Hercules glares at us like he hates the world. I quickly look away from him, choosing to do the wise thing by pinning my attention back on Clive, who I suspect is single and a man whose family isn't feuding with mine.

*Good choice, Paisley.*

*He's a good choice.*

---

WHILE DANCING, CLIVE OFTEN LEANS IN TO ASK ME loads of questions. He likes being close. Although I've decided to forget Hercules, I can feel his eyes on us. It has taken a lot of willpower not to test my supposition and turn to see if I'm right.

"What do you do on the weekends?" Clive asks, his breath once again warming my ear.

"Not much. Work."

"That's no fun," he remarks.

There's no need to tell him that I'm the poster child for *no fun*.

He asks me something else. With each question, he gets closer and closer. When he steps back to shuffle from side to side, I take a good look at him. Clive is classically handsome. His hair is dark and has a windswept appearance like Hercules's. His chin is square, and he has sexy dimples that are more pronounced when he smiles, also like Hercules. But Hercules is an inch or two taller than Clive. Essentially, if it were just his looks that drew me so strongly to Hercules, then Clive and I could skip off into the sunset. But it's not his looks that attract me. It's his essence. It's everything he exudes. I can't believe I ran into him tonight. Seeing him makes everything I ever felt for him come back stronger than when we were kids. I thought over time those feelings were supposed to diminish. Apparently, not in my case.

The song ends just as Clive says, "We should go out sometime. I'd like to get to know you better."

Hot and sweating from dancing, I fan myself with my hand. I decide that I'm not in the market for a new boyfriend simply because it's going to take at least a week or two or three to reset after seeing Hercules. So I put my hand on Clive's hard chest. Mouth near his earlobe, I say, "Thanks for the dance."

He gently takes me by the elbow. "Are you coming back?"

I force a smile. It would be easy to lie. But I've been taught to tell the rot-gut truth, even when the answer could shatter someone's heart.

"No," I say. "But again, thank you."

Clive looks shocked. I can tell he's one of those guys who isn't used to being turned down. I wish I could give him my number to put him out of his misery, but the last thing I want is to be pestered by a guy I'm just not that into. So I press my lips into a conciliatory smile, put my head down, and walk away from him.

Amy's voice blares through the speakers as I slip past partygoers focused on her. She's repeating the date, time, and address of the first rehearsal dinner before everyone gets too drunk to remember.

I keep my eyes on the floor as Amy makes an offhand comment about how the open bar was a bad idea and if Lake had known anything about these sorts of parties, she would have toned down the night's activities.

"Don't you people have to work tomorrow?" Amy asks.

Deathly silence is her response.

I'm relieved when I make it to the elevators. I take a quick look over my left shoulder. I'm out of sight in the short hallway. As I push the button to go down, I think that I probably should have said goodbye to Hercules.

But then, maybe not.

*Definitely not.*

I stare, unfocused, at the numbers above the elevator as they climb higher. Lake has reclaimed the microphone from Amy and is encouraging everyone to dance and drink like there's no tomorrow.

I chuckle at Lake as I think about how seeing someone makes certain memories return as though they happened only yesterday. When I ran into Hercules at that New Year's Eve party, I was with my roommate Eden, the younger sister of my cousin Treasure's friend. Being a Grove meant I could afford an Emerald Suite at AIT University and be all by myself. But Treasure insisted I take in a roommate, convinced that if I didn't, I'd end up being the loneliest girl on campus.

I hate to say it, but Treasure might have been right. Eden never let me sit around and be bored for too long. And she certainly wasn't going to allow me to sit at home, binge on ice cream, and watch New Year's Eve celebrations from coast to coast play out on TV. So she dragged me to a party near Harvard's campus. And there, while I was ordering a Coke at the bar, I found myself standing next to Hercules Lord.

Hercules and I admired each other back then just as we did tonight. I was wearing a black dress that belonged to Eden. It was so short that I had to constantly tug the hem down when I walked to keep my crotch and rear covered. I was miserable in that dress until Hercules's lustful gaze passed over me twice.

We looked into each other's eyes and smiled, and he said—just as he did tonight—"PG."

Hercules and I have natural chemistry. There's no denying that. However, there's also no denying that it would be difficult for us to have a normal boyfriend-girlfriend relationship. My family might disown me if we did. He would probably be disowned by his family too. Even though the hate is preposterous, it is real.

I yawn into my hand as the elevator arrives and the doors slide open. As I enter and search for the L button, I dream of falling into bed. I'm exhausted. I had more fun than I'd planned by dancing with Lake and then Clive. I probably shouldn't have ditched Clive the way that I did. Pressing the lit L button, I feel bad about that. He was such a nice guy. I expel a slow and comforting sigh as I lean against the wall.

Before the doors can finish closing, they slide open again. Leaning against the steel frame of the elevator, displaying the grin that should be trademarked, Hercules Lord asks, "Leaving early?"

# A Walk to Remember

PAISLEY GROVE

I pick my chin up off the floor, swallow the extra moisture pouring into my mouth, and breathlessly say, "Um, yeah."

For some reason, I feel as if I owe him an explanation. My mind lists all the reasons why I'm leaving way before the party's over, but I'm too tongue-tied to say any of them.

"Can I join you?" Hercules asks, his lips quirked up into an enticing smirk.

He steps into the car before I'm able to answer. Then, eyebrows raised, he raises the tip of his finger and lets it hover over the L button. *He's waiting.*

"Sure," I reply in a nervous, high-pitched voice.

His strong finger smashes the button. I'm reeling on the inside and hoping that it doesn't show on the outside as we drop down to the lobby. Silence hangs between us like forbidden fruit. I think he, too, is wondering who's going to speak first.

I so badly want to ask him to explain his relationship with Lauren. But it's clear they're a couple. So instead, I ask, "Getting some fresh air?" Because for certain Hercules Lord isn't leaving his girlfriend alone at a party to pursue me. I never thought he'd grow up to be the kind of guy who'd do that.

His appealing smirk hasn't gone anywhere. "Is that what we're doing?"

*Huh?* My eyebrows flash up. "I'm going home. But..." Out of curiosity, I tilt my head. "Are you insinuating that you're following me?"

"Yes, I am," he smoothly says.

I jerk my head back. "But you're not leaving without your date."

Amusement shows in his glistening eyes as they skip around my face. "Was that a question?"

*Great. He's flirting.*

I cock an eyebrow. My heart feels like it's in my throat. "That was a statement."

Hercules shoves his hands into the pockets of his black dress pants. They fit him so well that I have to avoid peeking at his package when he says, "Lauren will be fine."

"But she's your date."

He shrugs indifferently. "It's complicated."

"What's complicated about it?"

Smiling at the down-counting numbers, Hercules nods. "Ah... I remember that about you."

I frown, confused. "Remember what?"

"You're direct, PG. I've always liked it. When you talk, you never leave a guy guessing. But first, I gotta get you to talk."

I ponder his observation about me as the elevator comes to a stop and then opens.

Not once losing the charm in his smile, Hercules shoots out an arm and points his head toward the lobby. "Ladies first."

---

WE STAND IN THE LOBBY, FACING EACH OTHER. Maybe he's just as confused as I am about how to proceed.

Leaning forward and then tilting his head—one sexy gesture—Hercules asks, "So, where do you live?"

"Not that far away," I say breathlessly. *Damn. I*

*answered too quickly.* His nearness has spiraled me into sensory overload. I've lost control of my emotions and reason.

"Really?" He sounds very surprised. "Me neither."

"You live in this neighborhood?" I ask in a high-pitched voice.

His flirtatious smirk doesn't waver as he stuffs his hands into the pockets of his nice-fitting pants. "Yes, I do. And I'm not surprised. I seem to find you wherever I land. Boston or New York, all roads lead back to you, PG."

*Breathe,* I remind myself as I think back to our encounter in Boston. Also, I can't believe he just said what he said to me. *Is he flirting?* There's no way he's flirting. A gorgeous and strapping man like Hercules Valentine doesn't end up with a confused nerd like me.

"Yeah," I breathe, casting my attention to the black-and-white medallion-marbled floors and trace the circular pattern with my eyes. I want to insist that he goes back upstairs and enjoy the party with his beautiful date.

"Listen, PG," he says, regaining my full attention. He closes just about all the distance between us. "I've been wanting to say something about that night in Boston."

My lips part as I fight the urge to be flippant and say don't worry about it, what we did was no big deal. But the night was a big deal for me, a *very* big deal. I know discussing it with Hercules will bring me some peace about what happened between us.

"Yeah, I guess, we should talk about it," I whisper, feeling my face warm. *Damn it, I bet my skin looks all patchy. He can tell that he's making me nervous. I hate that.*

Hercules's eyes narrow just a touch as his gaze washes over me. I'm under his spell and I shouldn't be. I need to keep my wits about me. There are too many mysterious elements surrounding him, his relationship with Lauren being the biggest.

"Are you walking home?" he asks.

"Yes," I say in a strained voice. I clear my throat. "I mean, yes." *That was better.*

Leaning in, he asks, "May I escort you, then?"

I glance nervously over my shoulder, catching a glimpse pf our images in the mirrored walls between the elevators. "But what about Lauren?"

"She's not my girlfriend, PG. Relax."

I grimace. "But she's your date, isn't she?"

"No. Not really."

"Not really?"

Hercules sighs as if he's being emotionally drained by our back-and-forth. But I cross my arms, refusing to leave with him if he doesn't stop being dodgy about Lauren.

"She's my cousin," he says.

I jerk my head back in shock. "Oh," I say, relieved. *Why was that so hard to admit?* Then I think about the way she stuck to him as if she were metal and he, a magnet. "Kissing cousins?"

Hercules snickers at my probing joke, and puts a hand on my back, guiding me to the drum of the revolving doors. "There's never been kissing or anything sexual between us. Now, let's walk. Get some fresh air."

How can I resist him now? Eight years later and Hercules and I have yet again run into each other at another party. Yet again we're single. My body shifts into overdrive as I let him guide me to whatever comes next, and anything is possible.

---

OUR PACE IS SET AT A CASUAL STROLL. OUR WALK has just started, and I'm wondering whether I should speak first. In my mind, I can hear Max saying that she who speaks first controls the conversation. That's my brother, though—he's all about control. I'm not surprised Hercules noticed how direct I can be. With Max as a brother and Xander as my father, I don't have the luxury of being frivolous with my words. Nor do I have the patience for it.

"What are you thinking?" Hercules asks.

I stop staring at the stained cement and conclude that it's best that he start the conversation. I want to hear what he has to say about Boston first. "I'm thinking about a lot of things. But you mentioned the last time we saw each other," I say in an effort to pass the baton back to him.

Hercules grunts thoughtfully. "Yeah. About that night… why did you leave?"

I'm surprised he started there. "I don't know," I finally say with a sigh. "I was young, embarrassed."

"Embarrassed about what?"

I look up at him. *Is he really going to make me say it?* He seems to be observing every minuscule change in my expression.

Hugging myself tightly, I stare at his sexy lips. A strange sensation comes over me. I almost feel as though I'm falling into his mouth. My lips so badly want to mug his. That night we made love, we left the New Year's Eve party together. Eden almost didn't let me go off with him, but I assured her that I knew Hercules Lord from high school, so she stopped being a worried friend and let me go. His hired car drove us to his penthouse. We made out in the back seat on the way. I shudder, recalling how Hercules's cock rubbed me to orgasm several times before we arrived. He was getting off, too, taking himself close to the point of no return and then stopping himself from coming.

Endorphins pumped through our bodies, and our legs were wobbly as we walked into the building. We stared at each other with hungry eyes as we rode up to his penthouse in his private elevator. We were making out feverishly before the doors opened. Then we kissed all the way to Hercules's bedroom, where we rolled around on his mattress, touching, petting, squeezing, rubbing, and coiling our tongues deeper into each other's mouths. It was as though we were making up for all those days during our senior year of high school when we purposely kept our distance from each other.

There weren't many opportunities to fill him in about my virgin status before we did it. My panties were soaked, and I was so scared when he pressed the tip of his enormous cock against the entrance of my sex. *Tell him*, my brain kept shouting.

"Are you on the pill?" he asked.

I lied and said I was. I didn't want anything to stop the forward progression of something that I'd always dreamt of—Hercules Lord being my first.

Then his heaviness was on top of me and his face close to mine. His scent overpowered my senses. And the taste of his kiss—I was so overstimulated that I had to take deep breaths through my nose to keep from passing out.

When it happened, it hurt—burned like fire racing through me. But after a few gentle pumps, it wasn't so bad. Treasure thinks it didn't hurt as much as it should have with a man Hercules's size because I was so aroused. I showed her how big he was by pressing my two thumbs and forefingers together to form an O.

Suddenly, I remember something. Hercules has been frowning at my face for a few seconds. *I was clinging to him like a scared kitty. He knew...*

"You knew I was a virgin, didn't you?" I ask.

His eyebrows pull together then release as he stares ahead. I wait for him to say something. But now the city is doing all the talking. Car horns, brakes, and the general rumble of indecipherable noises rise like the city's personal theme song.

"I thought so, maybe, when we started. I know I'm pretty…" He turns his toothy, alluring smirk on me, and I skip a breath. "Robust."

I snicker, blushing, and nod. "I actually woke to pee, and I saw the blood I left on your pristine white sheets and panicked. I mean, obviously, if I was a virgin, then I lied about being on the pill. I was really ashamed about that. I didn't want you to see me as a liar, I guess."

He's silent for a while, and I feel as I did that night—like I'm about to pass out. Then he graces me with a courteous expression. "It was okay. You know?" His smile makes me simper.

"Thanks. But I was young and easily embarrassed about those sorts of things. Now I get that I should've stayed and dealt. I mean, I was playing with fire. No condom. No pill. I could've gotten pregnant."

He grunts thoughtfully. "We could've dealt with that."

I jerk my head back. "Oh yeah? How?"

"I would've been with you every step of the way, PG."

*Wow, the thought of that…* I tilt up my head and

38

take in his gorgeous profile. "You mean through nine months of pregnancy?"

"And beyond."

That makes me feel good, but I scoff anyway. "Our families would've torn each other apart."

Hercules tosses his head back to laugh. "Maybe, but if we had a child, that might've forced them to get along." He winks at me. "Like we get along."

I fold my arms closer to my chest, feeling the tightness in my shoulders. *Why do I feel so exposed?*

"So, PG, are you married? You're not wearing a ring."

*Oh... he checked.* I shake my head.

He grunts, intrigued. "Do you have a boyfriend?"

"No." I grin, preparing him for my impending stab at humor. "Besides what looks like a very incestuous relationship with your cousin, do you have a girlfriend?"

His eyebrows furrow as he grimaces as if a bitter taste has invaded his mouth. "No," he finally says.

I tilt away from him. "Are you sure?"

He chuckles. "I'm sure. But how are you single? A woman who looks like you, with your credentials."

I find that funny. "My credentials?"

"You're obviously beautiful—sexy, even. But you're profoundly smart too. Kind. Down to earth."

"What about you?" I ask. "You're tall, strapping, handsome, insanely rich, and it shows. And you're also kind, gracious, down to earth…"

We pass a restaurant. I turn after hearing a table of women giggling. I was right. They're reacting and admiring Hercules's assets.

"See," I say after we pass.

I love it when he tosses his head back and laughs. His Adam's apple and perfect profile make him look so sexy.

"About that night…" he says after his laughter has simmered into a delightful smile.

"Yeah," I sing, feeling happier than I have in a long time.

"I've been with plenty of girls before and after, but none of them were quite like you."

I aim my radiant smile at the concrete as my heart does a happy dance. "What do you mean by that?" I ask as we stop at the corner, waiting for the walk light.

No one else waits with us. No cars are coming, so they all jaywalk. Any other time, I would cross the street with them. However, Hercules and I don't move. We are obviously trying to delay our arrival.

Hercules rubs the back of his neck. "It was different with you. All of it. The kissing. The touching." He cuts a tiny smile. "The rubbing."

A knot forms at the back of my throat. *Oh my God, he remembers our car ride and how we sort of had dry sex on the way to his place.*

"I wonder…" he whispers.

It feels like the entire city has disintegrated into black matter, and there's nobody here except Hercules and me. I swallow nervously as he brings his lower lip into his mouth to moisten it. "Yeah?" I whisper.

Hercules reaches down and takes my hand in his. The walk light flashes green. But we stay put as he carefully draws me against his rock-hard body. I put up no resistance, sinking into his embrace.

"I've been wanting to do something since I first saw you."

I think I say, "What?" I'm sure I say it. I think.

Our deepened eye contact is akin to foreplay. My lips ache for what's to come. And then, slowly but surely, our mouths come closer and closer, savoring the delectable sensation. Our lips push against each other, then his warm tongue rounds mine. Everything feels like I'm surrounded by satin —our kiss, his hand gripping the nape of my neck, and my floaty head. Hercules and I have something in common when it comes to this. I have kissed other guys, but none of them had the ability to take me to where I am now.

"Um…" The sound escapes me as our relentless tongues make our kissing more fervent. My nipples are on edge. I'm creaming, squeezing him tighter, wanting more, more, and even more.

"Paisley," he whispers after he breaks our mouth contact, his eyes closed. "I live there."

It takes me a moment to get my bearings and follow his pointing finger. My eyes open a fraction wider when I see my building. "Oh. You're next to me. Well, my parents."

*What a crazy coincidence.* I am about to tell him that when he asks me over to his place for a drink.

# No Stopping Us

PAISLEY GROVE

I t happened again. As we walked the rest of the way to his building, my legs felt wobbly. My body is still pumping dopamine like a pumping jack. I vaguely remember the warm lights that surrounded us when we entered Hercules's building.

Now my back is against the smooth white stone wall of his private elevator. The atmosphere is erotic with blue light playing against the white. Hercules is gripping my forearms, holding my arms over my head, pressing them against the hard and smooth surface. His solid front is flush against mine. Our molten kissing takes my breath away.

"Your lips," he whispers before his tongue dives deeper into my mouth. The delicious sultriness and spiciness of our intense kissing makes my head woozy. I feel as if I'm floating on cloud-nine.

Then, Hercules's forehead presses against mine as he whispers, "Sorry."

Eyes closed, I swallow, failing at controlling my lust, I whisper, "Sorry for what?"

"Moving too fast."

My eyes flutter open. He's watching me. Our chests rise and fall in unison.

He swallows audibly. "I promised you a drink. I think you should have one. *We* should have one."

I nod. "I think so too."

---

HERCULES HAS TAKEN ME TO WHAT HE SAYS IS HIS favorite room in the penthouse, a den with south-facing views. He's already poured our drinks—a vintage Malbec for me and a Tom Collins for him. We've had a couple of sips of our cocktails. We sit comfortably on a white rug that's as soft as a slinky kitty, at the foot of a white leather L-shaped sectional. I luxuriate in the moment and mull over something Hercules said.

My eyes caress a scene worth millions of dollars as I behold skyscrapers extending to the edge of

Battery Park and then capturing the bay and New Jersey beyond. You miss nothing from being up this high. Even though I see these sorts of views from my parent's place, Hercules's views and his penthouse are more stunning. He's made himself a young, hot bachelor's paradise. His furniture is modern and sleek, with sharp lines and upholstered with expensive muted fabrics. And the distinctive light fixtures are beyond. I look up at the one hovering above us. It's cylindrical and emits warm orange light. The wine, the scenery, the lighting, and Hercules all put me in a sultry mood.

"Well, I wasn't going to go," I say, raking a hand through my hair. I'm referring to that fateful New Year's Eve party where we last ran into each other.

Hercules raises his knees and sets his forearms on top of his kneecaps as he swirls the ice in his glass. "Humph," he says thoughtfully. "Me neither. Nero"—he looks at me as if that name should ring a bell—"my cousin, who met your friend at the party. He insisted I get out and do something."

I frown, faintly remembering the guy Hercules was with. His name was indeed Nero. The next morning, when I crept back to my dorm, my roommate Eden hadn't returned yet. When she finally made it home, the new day had bloomed, and she never looked happier. We made ourselves comfortable on my bed as she told me all about the dreamy hours she spent with a guy named Nero. She also said that she hadn't given him her real name, especially after learning that he was a Lord.

"Too rich," she said, squishing her nose like she couldn't stand the smell of people with that much money.

"My family's wealthy," I said, rightfully feeling defensive. "My family works hard for every penny. That doesn't make us bad people."

She sighed as though my response made her weary. "I know that Pais. But the Lords are pretentious, old money assholes, and you know it," Eden had said.

I remained silent long enough to let the line of conversation drop. Because I hadn't known *it*. The only Lord that I knew was Hercules, and he was neither pretentious nor an asshole.

"What are you smiling about?" Hercules's oh-so-sexy voice brings me back to the moment.

I exhale softly through my nose. "Did your cousin ever learn my friend's name?"

Hercules hangs his head and laughs. He's in a very breezy mood, just like I am. "No. He wanted me to call you and ask for it. But…" He shrugs.

I nod. No words are necessary. That night so many years ago was a one-and-done experience. It was bad enough that we were together. If my family ever found out that Hercules was my first, they would go ballistic because he's a Lord. And of course, there was me lying to him about being on the pill. That haunted me for several days. For a few days, I found myself praying for my period not to come. But I also dreaded what would happen if Hercules had gotten me pregnant. My parents would've been disappointed in me. I could see Uncle Leo, my dad's brother and Treasure's father, looking at me as if I had betrayed my grandfather and made him turn in his grave. When my period finally came, I was relieved. I don't think I could've borne being the outcast of the family. I wasn't as strong then as I am now.

"Her name is Eden Castro." I take another sip of wine. "You should tell him. She liked him."

His thoughtful grunt feels like music to my ears. "Are you still friends?"

When I nod, my head feels buoyant. "Yes, we are."

He hums as if he likes that she and I are still associated with each other. Then he quirks an eyebrow. "Are *we* still friends?"

I am officially tipsy as I run a hand through my hair, smoothing my hair away from my flushed face. The wine is not only delicious—it's fast too. I'm less inhibited than usual as I look into his hypnotic eyes. "Were we ever friends?"

He snickers softly. "I thought we were."

"How so?"

"You saved my ass in Mr. Northam's class."

I raise the glass close to my lips. "Ah. High school. Yeah, we spent a lot of time together in the computer lab." I raise a finger pointedly. "Although you pretended to not know me outside of the computer lab."

He twists his sexy mouth thoughtfully. "But that went both ways."

My head feels so floaty when I nod in agreement that it doesn't seem as if I'm nodding at all. "But you were more popular than I was. If you'd spoken first, then I would've said something back. You, Hercules Lord, had all the power."

I close my eyes, easing the back of my head on the sofa as I wait for his response. I appear relaxed but I'm eager to hear his response.

But Hercules is silent for far too long, so I open one eye to see what's the delay. He's watching me with a steady, unreadable expression.

Now I open both eyes. "What is it?"

His lips hint at a smile. "Remember our conversations?"

*I'll never forget them.*

Nodding buoyantly, I set my half-filled glass of wine on a black coffee table that resembles a block of granite. "You said that you didn't like that your brothers treated you like a teenager. Even though you were a teenager." I chuckle softly, going with the floaty feeling in my head.

He winks sexily at me. "I was always a man before my time."

I hum, smiling. "I can't refute that."

Our gazes linger appreciatively on each other. He is incredibly handsome. I also relish in the ease of our conversation, and him flirting with me and me flirting back.

His finger traces my eyebrow and trails down the side of my face. I release the breath I've been holding while his finger completes its journey.

Suddenly he sits back as if he wasn't aware of what he was doing. "You missed your grandfather," he whispers and then clears the frog out of his throat. "And you hated New York City, which is why I'm pleasantly surprised you still live here. How did you put it?" He shakes his finger as his eyes taper thoughtfully. "It smells like the city dump."

My shoulders shake as I snicker. "It's an exotic aroma, isn't it?"

Hercules chuckles.

"But..." I sigh. "New York is like a rough and gruff boyfriend you fall in love with over time."

He grunts inquisitively. "Then you like your men rough and gruff?"

Laughing, I shake my head. "Not at all."

"Then how do you like us?"

"Seriously?"

"Yes."

I sigh energetically as my gaze wanders across the face of the man that I compare every possible love interest I ever meet to. I want to say, "I like them just like you, Hercules." But I can't say that. It's too early in our reassociation to admit that. So I let my body sink low enough that I can once again rest the back of my head on the sofa's cushion. "Oh, Hercules, I have classic daddy issues. Although I'm pretty sure being attracted to a man who has the qualities of my dad has served me well."

"Oh yeah? How so?"

I shrug. "First of all, my dad treats my mom as

though she's made for him, and he for her. He's also ambitious and strong and knows how to conquer while remaining a good person. Of course he likes things done his way, but he's fair. He'll listen attentively to a different point of view and make the necessary adjustments to his tablet of beliefs if he's been persuaded." I'm smiling to myself thinking about my dad. "Even though he drives me crazy sometimes and has been prone to overstep my boundaries for my "greater good" there are so many reasons why I admire him."

"Xander Grove?" He sounds utterly surprised.

I look up from my lap and at Hercules. He actually seems pleasantly surprised. "Yes."

His smirk is delicious. "Then I can't wait to meet him."

I raise my eyebrows warily.

Reading the expression on my face, Hercules laughs. We both know that's easier said than done.

Then I raise a finger. "Oh, and my grandfather. Everything I said about my dad, I can apply to him." I stop short of saying, "When he was alive." I like to think of my grandfather being alive in my heart.

Hercules grunts as he takes a big swig of his cocktail. There's a tone to the sound he just made. I can't quite put my finger on it, but it sounded a lot like judgment. But I know that if he and I are going to hang out, it's best to not talk about our families too much. We have always been able to avoid the strife between the Groves and Lords. I want to make sure we continue doing just that.

He clears his throat. "Well, I'm sorry about how I treated you when people were looking. If I could do high school over again, I'd do it differently."

I adjust to sit on one hip, facing him. I'm consumed by the ease and comfort between us. "What would you do differently?"

"I'd let everybody know that I liked you, for one."

When I smile, my insides feel all lit up. "You liked me?"

His gaze spreads across my face like a warm breeze. "I liked you a lot."

"Like, romantic interest 'like'?"

His chuckle titillates my insides. "Yes, romantic interest 'like.'"

I hum with delight as I fight the urge to stroke his bulging bicep. We've become too intimate with each other. This night is crazy, and unreal. Something that has been a long time in the making is happening between us. We're crossing the line. And

I'm not taking a step back, and apparently, neither is Hercules.

"I had no idea," I finally say. "I mean, you were very popular. Captain of the rowing team. Every girl in school had a crush on you, especially Greenly Rothschild." I roll my eyes, vaguely recalling her teenage face in my head.

"Ah, yes, Greenly." He takes a sip of his drink. "I forgot about her."

I softly jerk my head back in surprise. "Wasn't she your girlfriend at one point?"

His desirous gaze caresses every part of my face, and then he whispers, "She was never my type, PG."

That look he's giving me makes my heart thump like a bass drum. I raise my left eyebrow. "But she was the prettiest girl in school."

"Ha!" He puts his glass on the coffee table next to mine. "You were and are prettier than she'll ever be. And you're smart as hell. When you used to talk computer lingo in class, that turned me on."

I toss my head back and laugh. "It's hard to believe that talking C++ and functions made you sexually excited."

"Very," he says in a voice thickened by lust.

Unthinkingly, I let my eyes veer down to his hefty bulge. *Damn.* He's hard right now.

Then very carefully and slowly, Hercules leans toward me. My lips part as my chest rises and falls with my deep breaths. I know what's about to happen next. Before long, our lips entwine.

"Umm," we moan as our tongues tangle sensually. He tastes like citrus, gin, and Hercules.

Then he ends the kiss to put his lips near my ear. "Can I have you, Paisley Grove?"

When he places a sensual kiss on my lobe, I breathlessly say, "Yes."

With ravishing hunger, his lips capture mine. Hercules binds his large fingers around my arm and methodically guides me down against the fluffy rug we're sitting on. He stretches my arms above my head. Even though I'm indulging in the taste of his mouth and the feel of his hardness on top of mine, I take note that this is the second time Hercules has held my arms this way. I never thought his sex style would be so possessive. With our sensual kiss deepening, I gladly submit myself to him yet again, body and soul. But then I squeeze my eyes shut tightly as a picture of Lauren whispering in Hercules's ear comes to mind.

"Wait," I say as Hercules liberates one of my

breasts. My eager nipple hates me for stopping him. It yearns for his mouth to cover it, his tongue to swaddle it, and his teeth to nibble it.

"What is it?" Hercules breathes heavily as his hungry eyes shift back and forth from my face to my breasts. Then his rigid hardness digs into my slit, reminding me what's important at the moment. The pleasurable sensation is immediate, causing me to spew a quick breath.

I want to say never mind and let him finish what he's starting, but instead, I ask, "You said Lauren's your cousin?"

"Yes." He sounds impatient.

"Then why was she so possessive of you?"

He groans. "Do you really want to talk about her right now?"

"If she's your girlfriend, then yes."

"Paisley, if she was my girlfriend, you wouldn't be here with me right now. I don't cheat on women I commit to. And I'm not nor will I ever be committed to her," he declares with a bite.

Gazing into his earnest eyes, I believe him. *Oh goodness.* I'm on the verge of giving myself to Hercules Lord for the second time in my life. I nod, giving him permission to take me in any way he desires. Plus, my eyes can no longer hold his attention. Hercules swallows as he seems hypnotized by my hard nipple that's being aroused even more by the sensation of his heavy breath blowing against it.

Without further delay, he sucks in as much of my 34C-sized breast as he can fit between his dimpled cheeks. I grab hold of his strong shoulders as his tongue and teeth stimulate my nipple, sending shivers of pleasure to my lady parts.

I exhale heavily against the fresh air in the room. I'm experiencing sensory overload as he lets go of my arm and allows his hand to slide up my inner thigh, parting them and then…

"Ha," I gasp as the back of my head pinches the soft fibers beneath us.

His finger rounds my clit, applying pressure that makes an immediate impact. I squirm with delight as I gnaw on my bottom lip.

"Baby, don't do that with your mouth, or I'm going to have to fuck you first," he says in a sensually gruff voice.

*Do what with my mouth? Oh.*

I release my lower lip, and his mouth immediately seizes it. And we're kissing again as he intensifies his stimulation. My whimpers and moans join our urgent, warm, wet kissing. I'm so overstimulated that I'm battling the desire to faint from too much pleasure.

When an orgasm sprouts through my core, I moan louder into his mouth. But as the overpowering sensation expands, I turn my head, ending our kiss, so I can feel it grow.

"Yeah, baby," he whispers as I instinctively incline my hips toward his finger work. "I love it when a woman knows how to get what she wants," he declares.

Emboldened by his claim. I angle my hips. "Ah," I cry to the high heavens, and my thighs compulsively shiver as the explosion I've been seeking occurs, and pleasure like no other spreads through my hood.

Standing on his knees between my legs, Hercules mutters a string of curse words as he snatches off my black bikini panties and tosses them over his head. Then, eyes narrowed, he slides a finger up and down my slit.

"Damn. You're so wet."

He's right. I am. I'm so turned on.

He eagerly undoes his belt buckle and unzips his trousers. Through my hazy gaze, I watch him stroke himself twice before sucking air between his teeth. He's just as humongous as I remember. *How could I have ever endured such circumference during my first time ever?*

"I can't wait." He slides a condom out of his pocket, tears it open, and rolls the rubber over his erection.

"Me neither." I sigh.

He's ready. Thighs separated, sex eager, I stiffen with anticipation. Then his girth presses against my entrance. Slowly, almost ceremoniously, Hercules slides himself inside me.

He shivers. "Oh shit." Then, in one swift motion, Hercules rolls me on top of him. My thighs straddle him. Grasping my ass, he shifts me against his cock. I'm so full of him that I can barely endure how good he feels inside me.

With my cheek pinned against his, he whispers, "I want this so much."

Me too—as my moaning is full of want and yearning. He's stretching me so wide. His thrusts feels so good. And when Hercules finally becomes overwhelmed by his own pleasure, he lets go of my hips to grip my waist. That frees me up to chase every sensation his prodding inspires.

But I must raise my head to see his face because something pleasing is also occurring within my heart. Our breaths colliding, we fasten our gazes on each other. Hercules grimaces as though he's experiencing pleasure too gratifying to endure. The look on his face is so vulnerable that my emotions are heightened.

"Damn," he says. "You feel so good, baby."

And so does he. I would say that if I could find the right words. Our shifting is in perfect harmony as I bite down on my lower lip, close my eyes, and wait for the sparks inside my womanhood to heighten and grow and…

I toss my head back and cry out when it hits me. Body convulsing, I fall forward, flattening myself against the man of my dreams, blowing breaths against his neck as my sex jerks against his cock.

"Good girl, PG," he whispers, stroking my back until I'm still. That was so damn intense. *I've never…*

"Umm…" I moan as Hercules's lips find mine.

Our kissing is voracious as he rolls me onto my back. Now it's his turn to get off, and I'm finally able to wrap my legs around his tapered waist. But his torso stays high as he watches his cock slide in and out of my wetness. "Shit," he repeats. "So —good."

Even though I already came, he still feels so good in every way imaginable. I'm transfixed by the intense expression on his face. It's the only expression I ever fantasized about. I can't believe being inside me is pleasuring him this much.

*Damn.* I close my eyes and let out a high-pitched cry as one of his strokes lands the most gratifying punch.

"You like that, baby?" He does it again and again.

"Yes," I'm barely able to get out before biting down my lower lip to endure what feels so good.

Soon, my lower lip is between Hercules's teeth, and then his warm, tasty tongue slides against it until our tongues curl and stroke each other just as passionately as his cock strokes me.

And then…

# Pillow Talk

PAISLEY GROVE

## ABOUT AN HOUR LATER

We stripped off the rest of our clothes and left them scattered on floor of the den. Then Hercules took my hand. He and I gaped at each other, raising our eyebrows, and naughtily smirking conspiratorially as he led me to his king-sized bed, which has a sexy black leather tufted headboard. We've been rolling from one side of his bed to the other and from the foot of the bed to the head of it, making out like hormonal teenagers. We tried having a conversation since there's still so much catching up on the past seven years to do. At certain moments, our lips would release each other so that we could gently brush our noses—our cheeks—our foreheads. The energy of our contact generates feels like supple velvet. I feel that way right now. My head is on its way to Mars. My emotions overwhelm me. I think it's the same for Hercules too as we put our foreheads together to catch our breaths. I'm certain we're making up for the numerous times we wanted to do exactly what we're doing now without feeling guilty about it.

"I'm going to put on a condom," he whispers.

*Forget a condom. I just want him inside me already.* I swallow, forcing myself to be rational during this lustful moment. "Okay?" I softly say.

Air cools my skin when Hercules's body abandons mine. My cells already miss his. *Dangerous, Paisley. Very dangerous.* Regardless of how uninhibited I feel, I'm still playing with fire.

But I ignore my inner warning system for now.

Hercules's gaze roams my figure as he slides on a condom.

"You're so fucking sexy," he remarks.

My eyebrows shoot up. It's still unfathomable that Hercules Lord wants me—the nerd he met in high school.

Now that the cap is on, he watches me with pressed lips. "What are you thinking?"

I start to speak, but then think better of it. I'm on the verge of telling him the truth. But for some reason, I'm too embarrassed to admit that he makes me feel insecure.

"Come on, PG, what's putting that crease between your eyes," he says as he lays down beside me.

I clear evidence of my lack of confidence away from my forehead. "Nothing." My high-pitched voice isn't at all convincing. Hercules kneads my thigh and I'm on sensory overload.

"Do you want to stop?" he asks.

"No," I say ardently.

With the tip of his soft finger, he traces a line up my sternum and between my breasts. I'm melting when his hand caresses my chin. "Good."

Our eye contact stays steady.

Why do I want to say I love you? I can't love him. I haven't seen him in seven years.

His expression is so earnest when he says, "I've missed you, PG?"

*Don't be afraid. Say it back, Paisley.* My eyes tear up when I confess, "I've missed you too."

And then…

## FIFTEEN MINUTES LATER

I lie on top of Hercules's bare chest as he strokes my hair. I recall how soft and hairless his chest used to be seven years ago. He has more hair now but not a lot. I kiss his smooth skin, and he moans as if my lips are tastier than birthday cake.

"That was good, PG. You're good." He almost sounds surprised by that. I'm certainly surprised by his claim.

I raise my head to gaze into his serious eyes. "I'm good at what? Kissing your chest?"

He chuckles. "Sex."

I raise my chin a few inches higher. "Sex? I can't be that good at it. I have no real experience doing it."

His eyebrows furrow. I've piqued his curiosity. "No?" he asks.

I lower my chin back onto his wide, rock hard chest. "No."

Hercules's hand slides up and down my ass. His cock is soft. He won't be getting hard anytime soon. The last time he came, he gave me everything he had. But I still feel possessed by him.

"Can I ask you something?" he says.

"Um hmm," I hum contently.

"When was the last time you had sex?"

I contort my mouth thoughtfully, trying to remember. "It's been a while."

"Really?" He sounds highly amused by my admission.

"Yeah. Really."

"Was it satisfying at least?"

A face comes to mind.

Hercules chuckles. "That bad, huh?"

*Oh, I'm frowning.* That's what memories of my ex, Boyles Bellingham, make me do. I tell Hercules what happened between me and the boyfriend from hell. I'd already broken up with Boyles but for some reason, when he rolled into the city last year for a professional convention, we had dinner and then sex. The memory of him inside me makes my mouth taste even more bitter.

"What did he do to make you feel that way about him?" Hercules asks.

"He was a cheater." My frown grows more pronounced. "I also believed he liked me because of my last name."

Hercules softly strokes my back. "Why did you think that?"

I sigh with dread as everything resembling

desire wants to leave my body. Whenever I think about Boyles, I feel unattractive, maybe because that was how he made me feel—like nobody wanted me, including him.

"I don't know. He used to say my full name whenever referring to me. Like, he would say, 'My girlfriend is Paisley Grove,' instead of just saying, 'My girlfriend is Paisley.'"

Hercules chuckles. "That's it, PG?"

"Other than not ever being able to keep his eyes to himself and of course, cheating. I mean, if you're going to screw around and lust after other girls, why be in a relationship? He might as well have stayed single."

"That's because we men can be selfish. For instance…" Hercules wraps me up in his arms, holding me closer to him. "He wouldn't have gotten to do this if he wasn't your boyfriend. He'd just be lusting from afar."

I grunt. "That's disturbing."

Hercules chuckles. "It's immature. And you've also always been beyond your years. I would say, Boyles…" His eyebrows crumple. "Was that his real name?"

Chuckling, I say, "Yep. Could you imagine being named after a soar that can cause gangrene?"

"No, I can't," Hercules replies, laughing.

I shake my head, picturing sitting with my ex in the dining hall while his gaze landed on all the pretty girls in the room. "I don't know. I used to think he had no idea he gazed at women the way he did. I think he had serious issues."

"That's very gracious of you to give him the benefit of the doubt."

All that's inside me melt as we beam at each other.

It's as if Hercules's face is the only thing in existence. When he rolls me over onto my back, my heart knocks in my chest. When he's on top of me, we slide our tongues into each other's mouths. Our kissing feels like a ritual that's part of a sacred ceremony. *Why do I always whimper when we kiss?* Our lip-locking deepens as he rubs his softened cock against my slit.

*If only we had paced ourselves.*

He gives me a final tender and heartfelt peck on the lips, and our mouths grudgingly separate. Hercules's eyes stay closed for a few beats as though he's still savoring my flavor. I swallow, unable to look away from his handsome face. I'm afraid to blink hard. Maybe being with him this away is a dream, one that I never want to wake up from.

Slowly, we begin to smile at each other until that turns into laughter.

"Isn't this sort of unreal?" I ask. "Us being together this way?"

Hercules nods, and I kiss him. "It is, PG," he says as if my kiss took his breath away.

"What next?" I boldly ask.

Hercules rolls over onto his back but puts a hand between my legs to stroke my inner thigh. His touch makes me drip with wetness. I never knew my inner thigh was such a hot spot. The sizzling sensations are making me hornier.

"I don't know," he finally says.

Something in his tone doesn't sit right with me. I almost want to pull away from his touch… almost.

"So, this is just sex between us, right?" That question alone puts a note of pain in my chest.

His breathing remains even, and he doesn't slow the tempo at which he's stroking my thigh. "Am I out of your system yet?"

"No," I whisper. I wish he was. That would make the conclusion of our one-night stand easier to move on from. "Am I out of yours?"

Staring at the phallic-looking light fixture above his bed, he says, "You've never been out of my system."

His words spread through my heart like a fan as I ponder his claim. It sounds so unlikely. I'm sure he's overstating his feelings about me because of the sexual intimacy we've been sharing.

I abruptly lie on my side and circle his nipple with my finger. When he tenses from my stimulation, I'm caught off guard. I think he likes what I'm doing.

"I still can't believe you liked me in high school," I say.

He sucks air between his teeth. "Well, believe it because I did," he whispers and then clears his throat. "I had a massive crush on you."

His nipple has gotten extra hard. Moisture pools into my mouth. I want to feel the firmness against my tongue. "But I was a massive nerd. And nobody liked me."

Hercules curls his strong hand around my fingers. "PG?"

I lift my eyebrows questioningly.

"You gotta stop," he says breathlessly. "Or else."

Smiling proudly that I made him horny without really trying, I say, "Or else what?"

I sigh as his fingers slide up and down my slit before drawing circles against my clit. Then,

Hercules slides down my body until a warm, steamy, and silken sensation laps my clit.

"Oh Herc…" I cry as the rest of his name gets trapped in my throat.

*It's time for round three.*

---

WE HAVEN'T CHECKED THE TIME, BUT IT'S LATE. Hercules and I glisten with sweat. That last round of sex was amazing. Hercules made me come until his cock got hard and ready to plunge into my wetness.

And now, the side of my face is where it loves to be, lying on his chest as I listen to his heartbeat. Hercules has the physique many men would kill for. And right now, it's all mine.

We've been talking about a lot for who knows how long. He wanted to know more about Boyles and why I chose him if he was so awful. The answer was easy. Boyles misrepresented himself when I first met him. The truth is, Boyles and I didn't stay together long. It only took about six months for us to figure out that we weren't compatible.

We've been silent for several seconds. I think

Hercules is no longer curious about Boyles.

"You know what happened between your cousin and my brother?" he asks.

My heart takes a nosedive as I recall the tragic Lord-Grove love story. *Why would Hercules mention those two at this moment?* I'm certain he's trying to send me a message. Perhaps he's indirectly letting me know that he and I are on the same road that will lead to a similar tragic ending. When I raise my head to see his face, Hercules is watching me intently, waiting for my answer.

"Why did you ask me about them?" I finally say. My frown is so severe that it feels as if the skin on my forehead will detach from my hairline.

He appears taken aback by my mood.

"You don't have to mention Treasure and Orion to put emotional distance between us, Hercules. I never pictured us going past... you know, this," I lie.

He rubs the side of his face. "Look, PG. I'm not putting emotional distance between us. But we both know how complicated it would be for us to start something serious."

I feel sick to my stomach because he's so very right. "I know," I whisper.

"But I like you very much."

I exhale vigorously through my nose. "I like you

too," I admit in a tight voice. I already know where this discussion is going. And I shouldn't stop it, even if I could.

Hercules touches his forehead like it hurts. "There's something I should tell you." He looks worried, and that makes me worried too. He's watching me with eyes that are speaking, but I have no idea with they're saying. That's why I focus on his parted lips, waiting for the first words to leave his mouth.

"Hercules!" a man bellows in a gruff voice.

Hercules and I quickly turn our widened eyes toward the hallway. Fortunately, the penthouse is large. Whoever just entered isn't close to Hercules's bedroom yet. I don't want to imagine the fallout from a Grove and Lord getting caught in bed together. He and I already know how that will end.

"Are you home?" the man calls.

The shock passes, and Hercules scrambles to his feet. I'm not so panicked that I miss the pure perfection of his nude body. As I've already accepted, I'm extremely sexually attracted to Hercules. I've never lusted after a man in this way. That's probably why I feel a deep sense of loss, knowing that the intruder's presence has brought our night, and the likelihood that we will make love again, to a grinding halt.

"Achilles? Wait," Hercules calls, hopping into a pair of pajama pants that he snatched out of the nightstand.

"What's going…?" Achilles says and then goes deathly quiet.

I hear Hercules pounding the marble floor of the hallway.

"Whose red dress is that?"

Now I panic. "Oh no," I whisper repeatedly. My dress and shoes are still in Hercules's den.

I can't be seen by Achilles Lord. I'm certain he can recognize me if he sees me. And if he sees me in Hercules's bed, he'll tell Max, who would scold me to no end. I like the fragile peace treaty that exists between my brother and me right now. It can be easily broken. And something like this would blow our fragile alliance to smithereens. When Max and I battle it out, our squabbles can be spirited.

"You have company?" Achilles blares as his voice and footfalls get closer.

"That's none of your business," Hercules retorts.

I can't let Achilles catch me. So I roll out of bed and look around the room for somewhere to hide. I spot an alcove, and not knowing where it leads, I pad across the floor and go wherever the warm, dim lighting leads.

"Are you finally warming up to Lauren?" Achilles asks.

My heart feels as if it has turned to stone, but I keep shuffling on the tip of my toes past a bathroom that resembles one found in a five-star hotel.

"You're letting yourself into my place now?" Hercules asks. His voice sounds farther away than Achilles's.

"I always let myself in."

I make it out of the hallway that's connected to Hercules's room. I have no idea where I'm going as I pad down a corridor with white marble floors. I can't believe this is happening to me. *If Lauren is only Hercules's cousin, why does Achilles wonder if my dress belongs to her? Did Hercules mislead me?*

Naked as a jaybird and praying I don't eventually run into Achilles, I pass a familiar room and then step back. It's the den, and it's empty.

My heart accelerates as I rush in, and quickly collect my dress and shoes. I know my way out from this room. I tune out Hercules giving his brother the business for invading his privacy. Achilles asks

Hercules why is he being so cagey about having company.

"Who the hell is she, then?" Achilles asks as if he's entitled to know who Hercules is screwing.

A sour taste pours into my mouth as I note that Achilles is behaving a lot like Max would. My nerves are poking me like sharp knives when I make it to the private elevator and smash the down button. I'm shaking like a leaf. Nothing happens as I keep stabbing at it. Finally, it dings, and the doors slide open.

"What did you just do?" Achilles's voice is getting closer, and so are his footfalls.

"Achilles, wait," I hear Hercules say before the doors finish closing and the elevator drops.

I'm moving steadily to the lobby. There's no time to breathe a sigh of relief. I hurriedly put on my dress, shoes…

*Damn it.* I forgot my cocktail purse.

# A Night Over

PAISLEY GROVE

T he next morning, I'm sitting in my office. The lights are still off because my head needs a moment to make peace with being awake. My elbows are on top of my desk, my shoulders curled forward, and my face buried in my palms.

*What a night.* It feels too surreal to be true. Fortunately, I don't need a key to access my parents' luxury penthouse, which is where I've been living for two years too long. My fingerprint granted me entrance at 2:11 a.m. when I made it home.

Walking into his brother's apartment without calling first at that hour in the morning took real gonads and a lot of entitlement. Yes, indeed—Achilles reminds me of Max.

I didn't fall asleep until three in the morning, maybe later. I was so worried about my purse being at Hercules's. My cellphone was in it. I planned to wake up at around six, swallow my pride, and then head over to Hercules's place to retrieve it. However, this morning, my purse was delivered to me with a note.

*Thank you, PG.*

That was all he said. Talk about an anticlimactic ending to a lovely one-night stand. At first his insensitive note made me fume. But then I thought it through. Maybe Hercules's distant words of gratitude were what I needed to hear. We let our passions get away from us last night. The fact that we both scampered to hide our sex-adventure from Achilles says a lot.

Recalling my harrowing escape, I blurt a laugh. Heck, I probably would have told Hercules I loved him or something if we'd kept going. We probably would have made love through the wee hours of the morning until the sun came up. I had no plans to leave anytime soon. I'm certain Hercules wasn't close to kicking me out of his bed either. We were comfortable together.

And I'll never admit this to anyone, not even him, but I feel that in his bed and in his presence is where I belong for the rest of my life. That's silly, though. Because he's a Lord.

Heaviness descends on my shoulders as I consider telling my parents something like, "Oh, and Hercules Lord is my date for Thanksgiving dinner." My parents would blow a gasket. Whenever they speak of the Lords, they do so in negative terms.

"Look at her," my mom once said while reading an announcement on her cellphone. "Priscilla Lord is always social climbing. What does she do all day besides plan elaborate parties for herself?" Priscilla Lord is Hercules's mother.

And our family is in constant litigation with them. We both own software-development companies. GIT or Grove Industrial Tech, our company, is a lot more successful than Lord Technical Innovations—LTI—which is their company.

*But why did Achilles question Hercules about Lauren? What was that about?*

I'll call Lake as soon as I settle in for the day. Maybe she'll be able to elaborate on why the relationship between Hercules and Lauren is so "complicated."

Suddenly, the stress of escaping Hercules's

apartment seizes me again, and I laugh. I barely made it out without being seen.

"What's so funny?"

That stern and lifeless voice makes me jump. I take my hands away from my face to glower at my tall, dark, and strikingly handsome older brother, Max, who's standing in front of my desk. Max inherited most of our supermodel mother's most impressive features—even though he mainly resembles our dad. Without trying very hard, he always looks so put together. Whenever we're together and women are around, they flirt shamelessly. He's been passed hotel room keys, naked photos, phone numbers, and on several occasions, mailed packages containing skimpy panties. His response to all the extreme measures women go to just to get his attention is simply to have no reaction at all. I've been asked many times, by interested parties, if he's gay. I can unequivocally say that he isn't. Max has very distinctive taste in women. Even though he always looks impeccable, he's not attracted to the same quality in the opposite sex. The only girlfriend he ever introduced me to had blonde dreadlocks and her favorite outfit was part of an endless collection of paint-stained, faded coveralls, which she wore with scuffed-up combat boots. She was an artist named Kiera, who talked while she chewed and never minded her posture. I liked her a lot.

At the moment, I'm staring at my brother because he hasn't said anything yet. He's just grimacing me as if he's trying to figure out what's wrong with me.

"And by the way. Could you knock, please?" I snap, remembering how Achilles just let himself into Hercules's private space too. It seems both of our brothers have an issue with respecting boundaries.

Max's eyebrows remain pinched. "What's wrong with you?"

I fling myself back against my seat. "Nothing. What do you want?"

Max sighs sharply. I think he's decided to leave well enough alone. "I'm double-booked this morning. I need you to sit in on an important hearing for me. But I'm not sure you're up to it."

I shrug indifferently, even though a pinch of anxiety races through me. For so many years, I've done exactly what he's told me to do, no questions asked, in the name of family solidarity. Those days are over, and we both know it, but still, when he says jump, something inside me wants to ask how high.

"Your call," I say, opening my laptop. "Plus, I have a day."

My full day features a lot of work, including correspondence with Lake about the signage for the company's annual Endow the World with Technology benefit, along with plenty of questions about Hercules and Lauren.

Max drops a manila folder on top of my desk. "I need you to appear at an arbitration hearing on behalf of the company."

I frown. *Arbitration?* "Is it a legal matter?"

"It's arbitration, so yes."

I check the time on the top right-hand side of my computer screen as I roll my eyes at his smart-aleck reply. "I'm already late getting things revved up this morning. Where's Leo?"

Leo is our uncle, our dad's youngest brother, who is co-CEO alongside Max.

"In Palo Alto. Just do it, Pais. All you have to do is sit and be quiet. Let the lawyer do all the talking."

I tilt my head, trying to get a read on Max. It's just so weird that he's asking me to attend an arbitration hearing. It's such a huge responsibility and totally out of my wheelhouse.

"What's this hearing about?" I flip open the folder,

frowning as I read the first document, which is Max's welcoming speech for an up upcoming benefit. I throw my hands up in confusion. "This is your speech."

"Don't you need it?" he asks.

"Yeah, but what does this have to do with the hearing?"

He turns his back on me, heading for the hallway. "Nothing. And don't say anything to the arbitrator. Allen will do all the talking."

I shoot to my feet. "Who's Allen?"

"The lawyer who's going to do all the talking." That's the last thing he says before he's gone.

Now that I'm alone again, I sigh and plop back down in my chair. "Whatever...Max."

Make an appearance, do no talking—I can do that.

---

AFTER CHECKING MY EMAIL AND SITTING WITH RU, my executive assistant, to go over our action items for the day, I'm finally able to make that call to Lake.

She picks up before the second ring. "Paisley, I was just about to call you. Like seriously, I was just about to tap your name in my contacts list. There's something I bet you don't know."

Her tone is alarming, causing me to sit up straighter. I wonder if she already knows that I left the party with Hercules—and that he may have lied to me about his association with Lauren. "What's going on?" I try to sound innocent.

"Have you read this morning's *Top Rag Mag* alert?"

*Top Rag Mag* is the gossipiest of gossip blogs on the planet. As a public relations director, I'm aware that they exist, but as a mature human being, I hardly ever read anything they publish, at least for purposes of personal consumption. Sometimes, I'm forced to read the tripe they write because of my job. Also, my cousin Treasure is often a subject of interest to them. I'm always curious to know what they'd written about her. She spent six years as a cast member on a reality show about young heiresses of New York. During that time, *Top Rag Mag* wrote about who she supposedly dated, broke up with, or was just outright banging. Most of the guys they said she was involved with weren't even her type. However, the magazine never caught wind of her relationship with Orion Lord, which I believe, serves as a referendum on their ability to accurately snoop out the truth.

"I don't believe anything *Top Rag Mag* reports," I say with a cynical eye roll. "But…" I'm on the verge of changing the subject. I want to get to the crux of I why I called her, especially since I only gave myself twenty minutes to make it to Midtown for Max's arbitration hearing.

"Well, you *should* read it," Lake says with a chuckle. "At least this particular alert. Because it's about you."

My jaw drops. "Me?" *Why me?*

# Surprise, Surprise

PAISLEY GROVE

ake texted me the alert. I'm transfixed by a video clip of Hercules and me kissing on the corner of Fifty-Seventh and Seventh. Whoever filmed us did a great job of capturing the blistering passion between us. We were going at it as if no one existed but him and me. I close my eyes to relive how light my head felt, the rapid beats of my heart and the way his mouth tasted faintly of champagne and spearmint. I release a shivering breath. Just reliving the moment was getting me all hot and bothered. Gosh, he's such masterful kisser. It's as if our mouths were made for each other.

"Oh my…" I finally whisper.

"Read the article, Paisley. It's a hoot," Lake says.

I'm glad she's finding this amusing, but my skin

feels flushed and my stomach queasy. It's only a matter of time before someone in my family sees this. *And then what?*

I brace myself and then start reading aloud.

> *Ooh, salacious...*
>
> *But that's Hercules Lord, and sources say that he's engaged to Lauren Mueller. And the lady in red he's tonguing—#getaroomalready—is not his fiancée.*
>
> *Who is she, you ask?*
>
> *Wait for it because the plot is seconds away from thickening.*
>
> *She's Paisley Grove, cousin of one of our favorite NYC party heiresses, Treasure Grove. Sources say that Paisley is the good girl, but do good girls suck face like that?*
>
> *Judging.*
>
> *Not judging.*
>
> *Just saying.*
>
> *Sources also say that the kissing couple's families are mortal enemies. Nobody knows why the Groves and Lords hate each other. If you're out there and you know why, give us a buzz, or shoot us an email. Inquiring minds need to know.*

*But don't wander too far from this developing story. The pages are only beginning to turn on what may become our own modern-day version of Romeo and Juliet.*

*Sounds salacious, doesn't it?*

*I know. So... who do you think wears Hercules Lord better? The beautiful Grove heiress—oh, and may we add, daughter of supermodel Heartly Rose-Grove—or the hot, young vixen who is allegedly Mr. Lord's distant cousin?*

*Yes. You read that right—distant cousin. It's an old-money thing that we common folk will only ever see as being oh so gross.*

*Comment below.*

"Don't read the comments," Lake warns before I scroll down to the bottom of the post. "People can be cruel. Just know that it's fifty-fifty."

Mouth stuck open, I'm speechless. At least I now know that Hercules wasn't lying about Lauren being his cousin. However, he lied by omission when he didn't tell me he was engaged to her.

Finally, I swallow. "So, Hercules is engaged to Lauren?" I ask in tight voice. The question makes my stomach queasy. I haven't eaten. I should eat. But I'm not hungry anymore.

"Yes. Although…"

Lake's dubious tone sounds like the last ray of hope. I readjust in my seat. "Although what?"

"I don't think he's happy about marrying her. There's some story behind it. Mason says he doesn't know all of it, but I think he does. But, I wasn't aware you and Hercules know each other."

My temples throb, so I massage the one on the left. There's no way I'm telling Lake everything about last night. By not disclosing the whole truth about Lauren, Hercules has put me in a cumbersome position. I would have never slept with him if I knew he was engaged, regardless of the reason why. And Achilles—if he reads what *Top Rag Mag* wrote, he's going to know that I'm the woman who shed her red dress in Hercules's den.

I groan as if every inch of my body hurts.

"Paisley—question," Lake says like she's being coy about whatever she's dying to ask me.

"What?" I ask, feeling strained.

"Did you hook up with Hercules after the party?"

With my eyes closed, I rub my eyebrows. The lie

is on the tip of my tongue. However, I'm sure my long pause says everything.

Lake sighs as if my silence is a burden. "Even though I know Hercules isn't in love with Lauren, be careful with him, okay? He's not a player or an asshole or anything like that. He's actually a really good guy. But he's controlled by his family. And you know those Lords. How did *Top Rag Mag* put it? They have their old-money ways."

THE CAB RIDE TO THE ARIES BUSINESS CENTER IS taxing. I shift uncomfortably in the back seat the entire way, trying to think my way through the mess I stepped into with Hercules. I must forget about him. So far, Max hasn't caught wind of the *Top Rag Mag* post, and apparently, neither has Treasure, at least not yet. I'm expecting a call from her at any moment.

I make it inside the building and rub my aching temples while riding up the elevator to the fifth floor. I yawn, even though I'm too wired to be sleepy. I think I've decided to keep some serious distance between Hercules and me. *I don't know though...* I haven't conclusively made up my mind yet. Last night was beyond amazing. But good sense says that our sexing days are over. No more making love. No more kissing. And frankly, I should never, ever see him again.

Plus, I should be angry at him. But—all of that sex we had... All of those orgasms we gave each other. The sensual and deep kissing. The gazing into each other's eyes. His skin on my skin. I sigh.

*Oh no. The wedding...* I'll probably run into him at Lake and Mason's wedding, but after that, never again.

I'm early as I walk down a wide hallway that carries the scent and shine of freshly waxed tiled floors. Other than me, the only person in the corridor at the moment is a man who's wearing an impeccable gray suit. I split my attention between the guy and the room numbers, trying to figure out if he and I are supposed to link up. He's standing in front of 1604, which is where I'm going.

*Is he Allen Sussex?* The closer I get to the man, the easier it is to see how familiar he looks, though. Light hair, clean-shaven square chin, he's classically handsome.

Upon recognition, I stop in my tracks. "Clive?"

He flashes me an easy smile. It's definitely Clive, from the party last night. He doesn't look surprised at all to see me. I suspect he's been expecting me. "Paisley Grove. Fancy meeting you here."

"Same," I say, purposely erasing my frown as I finish closing the distance between us.

"I'll be representing you for this hearing."

I casually tilt my head to one side. "But is your real name Allen Sussex?"

He chuckles. "No. Allen couldn't make it. So you got me. If that's okay with you." He's flirting, which only makes me remember my night with Hercules.

I'm on the verge of apologizing for not saying goodbye to him last night when the elevator dings so loudly it steals our attention. Clive and I turn to see who's joining us in the corridor. The doors slide open.

I take a sharp, inaudible breath as my jaw drops. I can't believe who I'm looking at.

## More of Her

HERCULES LORD

**W**hat a goddamn coincidence.

I swallow hard and tug at my tie to loosen it a bit. It's PG. *What's she doing here?*

Last night, Achilles let himself into my penthouse to inform me that he needed me to represent LTI at today's hearing. He caught wind that Max Grove would be pulling a fast one to delay reaching an agreement. My job is to stay quiet while our cousin Nero, the lawyer representing our company in this matter, battles it out with GIT's counsel. This hearing is all about securing our rights, at whatever percentage that will be, to TRANSPOT, which is 3D software that was first conceived and developed by my grandfather Hugo and their grandfather,

Charles Grove. It's a mystery why the men eventually fell out. Charles is dead and my grandfather is pretty reticent about clearly articulating what happened between thm. All we know is that Hugo, who had sunk millions of dollars into the development of TRANSPOT, stopped funding the project, and our programmers were expelled from the research team and acquired data was never handed over to my grandfather. Charles Grove, who by then had acquired enough wealth from other software development ventures, started funding TRANSPOT on his own. Over the years, we've heard rumblings that GIT was making remarkable progress on TRANSPOT. So Achilles and I took the matter to court and the court agreed that our grandfather, who had once been CEO of our company, still holds a certain percentage of ownership in TRANSPOT, and that's why we're here today.

Max's strategy is to force Dan Munster, the arbitrator, from conclusively ruling on the court set agreement, which gives us fifteen percent ownership of TRANSPOT. Max prefers we get nothing. And, built into the agreement is a ruling that states the final decision can't be made until an agent familiar with the development of the software is at the hearing and presents proof that Charles had reimbursed my grandfather the funds which were paid to him for earlier phases of research. Charles is dead, but my grandfather isn't, and Hugo insists reimbursement never occurred.

Nero thought Leo Grove, Charles' second son and Max's uncle, would be representing their side today. Max had earlier presented evidence that Leo has no knowledge of the development of TRANSPOT. Nero has found proof of the contrary and is prepared to argue that point so that the final ruling could be made today. But none of us could have guessed they would send Paisley. She's a good play on Max's part. Of course she knows nothing about TRANSPOT.

"Isn't that Xander Grove's daughter?" Nero asks, narrowing his eyes at Paisley.

"In the flesh," I say, distracted by how beautiful she looks this morning.

"Damn, she's beautiful."

"Yeah," I whisper.

Sex agrees with her. She's glowing. And she's wearing a sleeveless white blouse and a black skirt that shows off her hips and long legs. I pinch bottom lip and push my tongue against the roof of my mouth. My senses remember sucking on her breasts, kissing her mouth, and going down on her several times.

"Aw, shit. Tell me you didn't fuck her again?" Nero whispers.

I snap myself out of my daze to grimace at my cousin, who's apparently been watching me. "What?"

"You're pulling at your lip. That means you did. When? Recently?"

I press my palms down hard on Nero's shoulder and make sure he's looking me square in the eye. "Just tread lightly with her, got it?"

Nero's light eyes burn with annoyance as he shakes his head. "I'll do what needs to be done."

That's not what I wanted to hear. I turn to steal another view of Paisley. Seeing her gives me fuel to stand toe to toe with a gladiator like Nero. However, I now find myself trapped in her gaze as she and her lawyer watch us. All the blood has drained from her face. And her lawyer…

"Who is he?"

"Fuck," Nero mutters. "It's Clive Alden."

"Clive Alden," I repeat. "He was at the party last night. I think he's a friend of Lake's." Lake knows everybody—people from all walks of life. I joke about it with Mason sometimes, asking him how he could be the least social person on the planet, marrying a woman who knows just about everybody in New York City.

"It doesn't mean a thing, though. Alden is slightly better than Allen. Actually, it's better that he's here, and her too. I can make useful tools of them." Nero is eyeing the opposition like a snake does its prey.

I slap him hard on the shoulders again. "Don't screw with her, Nero." I said, "proceed with caution when dealing with PG. I'm warning you."

He shakes his head hard. "I almost forgot you have a nickname for her."

"Eden Castro," I say.

I give him a moment to process. Then his shoulders slump, showing that a kernel of the fight has left him. "Okay," he concedes. "Just get me her number."

I'm about to shake on it with Nero, but then Clive Alden puts his hand on Paisley's back as they head toward us. *He's touching her.*

"Hercules Lord." Clive's voice echoes in the hollow corridor.

She's walking now, so he can take his hand off her. But he doesn't. Of course. I bet it feels good to touch her. No doubt his cock is sizzling.

"Where's Max?" Nero asks, even though I suspect he knows the answer. "And Allen?"

They're in front of us now, and his hand is still on Paisley's back. I'm losing control, rolling my shoulders, rubbing behind my ear, fighting the urge to tell Clive that he can now remove his hand from... *What is she to me? My woman? The person I want to be my woman? Fuck it. She's PG.*

"I'm Clive Alden."

"I know who you are. Where's Max Grove?" Nero asks, insistent.

Clive remains as cool as a cucumber. "Max is out today. He has the flu."

Nero and I snort facetiously. He's lying, and Paisley's widening eyes prove it.

"We're playing it this way, huh?" Nero asks.

Clive's wearing a shit-eating grin as he inclines back, feigning ignorance. "And which way is that?"

Nero laughs, but there's no humor in it.

"Good morning, Paisley," I say. It becomes deathly quiet as we wait for her to respond.

Her eyes are cold as she glares at me. "Good morning." Her tone is cold too. She's never spoken to me that way. She must have found out the truth about Lauren and me. I'm certain she heard Achilles inquire about Lauren.

"Paisley," Clive says, turning to her, making sure he has her full attention.

She's not looking at me anymore, and the absence of her attention is driving me crazy. I have to talk to her alone and explain my obligation to Lauren in complete detail. I was going to leave a message about Lauren with her purse when I had the concierge return it to her this morning, but then I thought that would be too insensitive. I wanted to explain as much as I can about Lauren to her in person. All Paisley needs to know is that I'm never going to marry Lauren, especially now that she's back in my life.

Clive nods. "Remember my instructions."

"What were your instructions to Miss Grove, Alden? She's not supposed to speak to my client? They're old friends." Nero leers at Clive. "Very good friends."

It takes everything I have to stop myself from elbowing Nero for landing a nice punch. I like how his subtle insinuation that PG and I have gone beyond the friend zone has landed with Clive who is trying to pull himself out of his state of shock. However, on the flip side, Paisley looks horrified.

"Nero," I blurt, chastising him.

"I'm not calling this off, Alden," Nero continues. He's fired up, not giving a damn what I want. "Let's go fight."

Clive jerks his head back. "Oh, fight? Wow. I didn't know this was a schoolyard brawl. This is an arbitration hearing. This is about agreeing, not fighting."

Nero glances at me as if to ask, "Can you believe this guy?"

"May I speak to your client alone, please?" I ask. I want to talk to Paisley before Nero goes into that room and tries to rip her apart.

"No," Clive and Paisley say at the same time.

I focus solely on her. "PG, let me explain."

"Explain what?" Nero asks.

I'm staring into her gorgeous eyes, pleading with her. She quickly looks at the floor, breaking our intense eye contact.

"There's no talking to my client, and you know it, Lord." Clive puts his hand on her back again. "Let's go inside."

I smell her as she passes to enter the conference room. I tilt my head back, close my eyes, and massage the bridge of my nose.

I know we're alone when Nero asks, "What the hell was that?"

"Just let it be."

"Hercules, we're close, so don't fuck this up. You understand? I bet that was why he sent her. He must have known you would be here and that you had a thing for his sister. Oh… that fucking Max Grove. He's cunning as hell."

My head hurts as I glare at Nero who's shaking his head. His conclusion makes no sense at all. I should say something to set his mind at ease, but he's right to be worried. Max certainly didn't strategically plan to have his sister sit across the table from me. But it's just as it was in high school. Whenever Paisley Grove is near, I'm not at my best. She ruffles me. No other girl or woman has made me feel this way—like I want to experience her twenty-four seven. It's insane.

Finally, Nero takes me by the shoulders and makes sure we have solid eye contact. "I need you to concentrate on what we have to do today. Don't screw this up over a girl you can never have. Because we're close. We're on the precipice."

The thought of that sits in my throat like a lump of clay. *I can't have Paisley? Bullshit.*

I shrug his hands off me. "Let's get this over with." The faster it's over, the sooner I can have her all to myself.

# Us Against Them

PAISLEY GROVE

I feel like I'm stuck in a bad dream while having an out-of-body experience. It's not a nightmare because Hercules is my leading man, but the circumstances surrounding us are nightmarish. Clive has instructed me to not say anything else to Hercules or his lawyer. And if the arbitrator asks me to answer any questions, I'm to repeat, verbatim, "I am not acquainted with the details of this case. Please grant me the allotted sixty days to gain knowledge of the facts."

It's clear to me that this entire procedure is pure BS. Max may be comfortable lying and scheming to win, but I'm not. And I'm supposed to lie and say Max has the flu. He looked healthy this morning.

"I don't like this," I whisper to Clive. We're to

sit on one side of the table, and when Hercules and his lawyer enter the room, they're to sit across from us.

*But why does his lawyer look so familiar?* "His lawyer. What's his name?"

"Nero Lord." Clive sets his eyes on me. I'm thinking he wants to see how his answer landed. After a moment, he frowns as he slams his folder closed. "I'm worried that—"

The door opens. I'm mesmerized by Hercules as he walks in first. It's just so weird that I hadn't seen him in nearly eight years, and now he's back in my life in a major way.

"Just stick to the plan," Clive says.

I nod.

"And after this, let's grab something to eat and talk. Have you ever been to the Chest of Chelsea?"

I don't nod or say anything as Hercules and Nero sit down across from us.

"It's almost impossible to get a table, but I always get one," Clive adds.

His voice sounds as if it's many miles away. It's hard to be self-aware at the moment. Am I staring into Hercules's powerfully intense eyes? *Yes. I am.* And I'm experiencing this weird sensation of feeling as though I'm falling into him. It happens whenever

I see him. It happened last night and many times in the past. I've pondered why. *Is he my soulmate, or am I just so attracted to him that my hormones soar?* I often wonder I'll ever stop getting that feeling around him.

But for now, I remind myself that Hercules Lord is just one man. And according to *Top Rag Mag*, he's one engaged man.

I force my eyes off Hercules's face yet again when the doors behind him and Nero open. In walks a tall, thin man with a long face. He's leading a small middle-aged woman carrying a case and a younger man with a brown leather briefcase in each hand.

I sit up straight. I'm nervous. There's no escape. I have to go through with this charade. It's Clive and me against Nero and Hercules.

*That's just great.*

---

NERO HAS BEEN GOING ON AND ON ABOUT THE details of the case. I've been keeping my eyes pinned to his face. Nero is handsomer than I remember. He looked very young back when he hooked up with Eden—like a teenager. However, she said that Nero, like Hercules, was a student at Harvard.

Age has served Nero well. He reminds me of a young Tom Cruise, a preppy kind of guy with an edge. What's funny, though, is that Eden's a lawyer too. When they met during that New Year's Eve party, she was studying digital architecture. I was shocked when she told me she'd enrolled in law school a year after we graduated. Law is a large leap from digital architecture.

I decide to call her tonight and let her know that I saw him. She would be amused by it. I wonder if she's seeing anybody.

So far, I've pieced together an idea of what's going on from the legalese talk. There's some kind of rule in place that says that a member of my or Hercules's family can enter the arbitration process at any point if an appropriate excuse is given. Clive passed the arbitrator, Dan Munster, a doctor's excuse on behalf of Max. And since Max is out, I'm in, and that means I could be granted a six-month postponement to get caught up with the details of the case.

I've been biting my tongue, fighting the urge to expose the lie coming from my side of the table.

"Go on, Dan. Ask Miss Grove if her brother has the flu," Nero says.

Clive scoffs. "Now he's telling you what to ask my client?"

I grow stiff, hoping the arbitrator doesn't ask me to answer that question. But soon, I'm staring into Mr. Munster's serious, gray eyes.

"Miss Grove, are you aware of the details of this case?"

I turn to Clive, panicked. His eyebrows shoot up as he nods. I think I'm supposed to deliver the line he's been teaching me, but I can't remember it.

"No," I finally say.

Clive shifts uncomfortably in his seat and then starts shuffling through the pages in his folder.

"Would you like to know the details?"

My gaze lands on Hercules's face. Then I hear a tap and look down. The tip of Clive's finger is pointing at words on a sheet of paper.

I'm about to deliver them just as they're written, but then I purse my lips. Why shouldn't I know the details of what's going on here? I'm more than the PR director at GIT. My grandfather had bequeathed me a portion of the company which makes me fifteen percent owner. I also have lifetime royalties for Killer Firewall, software that I created for a coding competition in high school.

Dan's sharp gray eyes are waiting for me to say something. Curiosity may kill the cat, but I definitely want to know what this is all about.

"Yes," I say. My heart beats a mile a minute. *What have I just done?*

"Objection!" Clive roars.

"Denied," Dan retorts.

Nero glances at Hercules with surprise. Up until this moment, Clive has regarded me with smiles and flirtatious eyes. Now he's seething at me.

But I rip my focus off him and set my curious gaze on Dan, who relays details I never knew about the licensing claims the Lords have made regarding TRANSPOT. Then Dan asks me if I have knowledge of the product.

I'm on the edge of my seat. "I do."

The tip of Clive's finger slams down on the table. I'm aware that he's pointing at his carefully crafted response for me.

"Could you tell us what you know about the software?"

I consider all I've just heard. "Well, I didn't know the Lords had any claim to the licensing.

However, I do know that we're not even close to going to market with it."

"And how do you know this?"

"Objection," Clive roars.

"Denied. Answer the question, Miss Grove," Dan insists.

My neck feels hot. I think I should stop talking, but instead, I say, "As I stated, I don't think it's ready for market."

"Say it," Clive hisses, barely moving his clenched lips. "Say it now."

"Miss Grove, are you admitting that you have technical knowledge regarding TRANSPOT?" Dan asks, easily ignoring Clive's rebuke of me.

I'm on the verge of answering his question, but my eyelids come down as my grandfather's face comes to mind. My heart twists into knots, and I'm struck by the same numbing feeling that keeps me from jumping two feet into helping Max get back on track with TRANSPOT.

I'm not fully aware of what's going on, but I'm gasping. Every inch of me is gripped by a feeling of pain and loss. I miss Grandfather so much, and I feel as if we had just buried him yesterday. I'm coughing, trying to breathe easier.

Hercules makes his way around the table and

squats in front of me. He's stroking the top of my thighs. "In through your nose. Out through your mouth," he repeats.

I latch on to his soothing voice, attempting to steady myself until I'm able to do exactly as he says. Gazing deeply into Hercules's eyes, I whisper, "I am not acquainted with the details of this case. Please grant me the allotted sixty days to gain knowledge of the facts."

"Continuance, please," Clive shouts. He's angry, and all because of me.

"Okay. Continuance granted, but this is it. No more after today," Dan says.

"You want to take a walk?" Hercules asks.

Gazing into his concerned eyes is keeping me from falling apart. I don't realize I'm crying until he swipes the tears from one of my cheeks and then the other.

"We should go grab lunch and talk about what happened," Clive growls. It's clear by his tone that he's making a direct objection to Hercules asking me to walk with him.

But Hercules still has my full attention when he says, "Come on—walk with me, PG. Let's get some air."

# Let's Make a Deal

PAISLEY GROVE

T he mild sun warms my crossed arms as Hercules and I stroll up the avenue. Getting far away from that overly air-conditioned room and those proceedings is just what the doctor ordered. However, I'm embarrassed about my minor breakdown in the end. I have no idea where that came from. I must have some suppressed emotions that I'm not dealing with. Actually, I know for certain I have suppressed emotions that I do not want to pull to the surface.

"Better?" Hercules asks.

I glance at him, happy he's with me. I press my lips into a contented smile and nod.

"Good. I'm glad you're better." He studies me for a long while, and I can tell he wants to say something. We have Lauren to talk about, and I'm about to bring her up first when he says, "You were dancing with your lawyer last night at the party."

I've had enough conversations with Hercules by now to recognize that he had not asked a question but made a statement.

"He must be Lake's friend," I say. "I think she knows the whole damn city."

"He likes you, PG. But I don't like him."

I sigh, amused. "You can't be jealous. Like, seriously, you have no right to be."

We're in Midtown, heading east toward Eighth Avenue. Hercules continues watching me. He seems absorbed in his thoughts. "I'm sure you heard Achilles mention Lauren."

I'm relieved that he said something about his fiancée before I could. "I heard."

"Lauren and I are fifth cousins. And…" He squeezes his eyes tight as though he regrets what he wants to say next.

"You're engaged to her," I say, letting him off the hook.

"I am." All the breath seems to leave his body. "But who told you?"

"Perhaps you should've."

Hercules runs his fingers through his hair. "I was going to tell you."

"When?" I snap.

He's silent for a moment and then asks, "Did Lake tell you?"

Even though this conversation strikes me like a two-by-four to the head, I keep it together. "I'd better show you something."

I take my cellphone out of my purse and call up the alert Lake sent me this morning. We stop walking while Hercules reads it. Oddly, he's smirking, amused. Nodding while reading, he says, "That was good." Then his eyebrows shoot up as he glances at me.

I try to appear as unfazed by his brazen flirting as possible. I can't be taken in by Hercules's allure. He's engaged.

He hands my phone back to me. "I'm not engaged to her by choice, and I'm not going to go through with it."

He sounds so sure of himself, almost like he's hopelessly trying to convince himself that he's not obligated to marry a woman he apparently doesn't love.

"Then you're breaking off the engagement?" I ask, testing his resolve.

He looks bitter, almost angry as he glares ahead of us. "I've never officially asked her to marry me. I was just told I would. There's not even supposed to be a ceremony. It's all supposed to occur on paper. Not so romantic, is it?"

Frowning, I say, "You said 'supposed' twice."

Hercules barely shakes his head. He really looks angry about having to marry Lauren.

"Is that even legal?"

Hercules's jaw grows tense, and he watches me, blinking. The blood has drained from his face. And I've seen this worried expression before. He used to look that way a lot in high school.

"PG." He folds his arms. "You really don't understand what's going on here?"

I shrug. "I think I know. You marrying your cousin has something to do with money, doesn't it?"

We turn up Eighth Avenue. "I'm being coerced to marry her."

"By whom?"

He narrows his eyes at me as if he's surprised that I don't know the answer already. I do know the answer, but I want to hear him say it.

"By my family, PG. Marrying Lauren leverages the rules of the Lord Trust in our favor. I'm surprised you don't know about the stipulations of the trust. Your brother and uncle are quite adept at weaponizing the trust against us."

My face feels pinched. I can't stop shaking my head. I hate the way Max and Uncle Leo have run Grandfather's enterprise. However, I'm not sure I should share that with Hercules, even though it's probably written all over my face. No matter how much I love Hercules, he's still a Lord. That has always been the major factor that keeps us apart.

After a long period, the awkward silence does its job and puts his previous comment about my uncle and brother in our past.

Hercules snorts and shoves his hands into his pants pockets. "What would your parents say if you brought me home for dinner?"

*Whoa, that question came out of nowhere.* I pull the sides of my mouth down, visualizing the answer. I see myself walking into my parents' Greenwich, Connecticut, estate with Hercules by my side. They look mortified.

"It would be a disaster," I admit.

Hercules chuckles. "It would definitely feel like a disaster. But it wouldn't be a disaster because we'd be together."

I snort as I shake my head. "Do you ever stop?"

"Stop what?" he asks, flashing his charming smile.

"Flirting."

He throws his hands up as if he's innocent. "I'm not flirting. I'm merely stating a fact."

Our laughing together feels more like collusion than amusement. I raise an eyebrow, giving in to the fantasy of him accompanying me to a dinner with my parents. "I would do it, you know. Just to watch them squirm."

"Then it's a date."

We laugh.

Hercules drops his head and simpers. "I like this, Paisley—being with you." He lifts his head and stares deep into my eyes. "I don't want to stop seeing you."

I feel my heart beating in my throat as my facial muscles fall slack. I want more of Hercules Lord, too, regardless of his being engaged to Lauren. But having sex with him like we did last night would be a slap in the face to every woman—friend, family, nonfriend, and even Lauren. "I can't." That comes out in a thick whisper. I clear my voice. "I respect the girl code."

I'm not sure whether his grunt means he's

impressed or intrigued. "Then let's just be friends," he offers up.

I chuckle, realizing that Hercules is purposely downplaying how difficult it would be for us to just be friends, especially after last night. I can't stop craving a repeat. However, I decide to play along to see where we end up.

"But we are friends," I say.

"Better friends. Good friends. Indestructible friends."

When I turn, I already know that I will meet his charming smile. "And how do you propose we do that?"

"Let's hang out more."

I raise an eyebrow skeptically. "What do you mean by"—I draw air quotes—"'hang out more'? Is sex involved?"

His mouth goes through several anxious contortions before he says, "It doesn't have to be. We can do what we're doing now. Walk. Talk. Get to know each other better."

"What do you want to know about me?"

"What was going on with you in the conference room? Why did you break down?"

My smile drops. The game has taken a turn

onto a street I never thought we would travel down. My eyelids flutter closed as I inhale deeply.

Then I open my eyes, and taking in every part of Hercules's face, I whisper, "I don't know."

His eyebrows furrow. "Come on, PG. I think you do know."

I grimace, shocked that he said that.

"You're too smart to not know. You can't talk about it, but you should. It'll do you good."

My lips are pressed together as if on some subconscious level I'm defying him. But he's right. I do know exactly why I had that breakdown. I found some things after I graduated from college. They were hidden in a chest at my grandfather's mountain house in Aspen.

A pregnant silence grows between us.

"You don't have to tell me," he finally says.

"It's just…" I glower ahead. "I think it has something to do with my grandfather. I miss him. Even now, it feels like he was just here. Yet he's been gone for eleven years. And you know, I thought I'd be over my grief by now." I heave a sigh, but it's not strong enough to dispel my sorrow.

Hercules is quiet for a few beats. "You have good memories of him?"

"The best."

"Then hold on to them." All of a sudden, he stops walking and puts a hand on my back, causing a thrill to shoot through me. "Hey, do you want a doughnut?"

I frown at his perfectly handsome face and then turn to glimpse the rows of decorated doughnuts through the window where we just stopped. My mouth waters, but a force of resistance shoots through me. "You know what's funny and probably unbelievable?"

His white teeth flash past his kissable smile. "What?"

"I haven't had a doughnut since I was a kid."

He leans away from me. "Get out of here."

The longer he touches me, the more excited I become. I should probably step away from his hand. But I can't.

Swallowing, feeling flushed, I nod. "It's true. My parents never let me eat junk food growing up. Well, unless it was on a special occasion. Like my birthday or a Christmas party."

"Well…" He puts his mouth to my ear. "You don't know what you've been missing."

*Oh no. My lady parts just trembled. Can we really be friends without sex?*

Hercules opens the door to the shop. "One doughnut won't hurt," he says, coaxing me.

I stomp on that red flag that's waving inside me, telling me that my parents don't approve. I take a moment to realize that feeling this way is strange. I'm almost thirty. I wonder whether my parents really still have this much power over me. Then it makes sense, and I realize why Hercules would struggle so much about marrying Lauren. I know his family exudes the same amount of control over him. Since we're in it together—we might as well be in it together.

"Okay," I say, smiling and showing two fingers. "I'll have two."

Hercules's smile stretches wide. I love making him smile that way.

"Now, that's the spirit, PG."

---

HERCULES BUYS A HALF DOZEN OF THE DOUGHNUTS the girl behind the counter says are her favorite. He's a natural flirt, but there's nothing sexual about the way he goes about it, at least not toward her. The girl, however, basks in his charisma. Then, when their transaction concludes, he sets all his focus on me and me only.

I realize this is the first time I've been out in public with Hercules as an adult. In high school, when we would meet after school to work on our computer-programming project, I never paid attention to whether Hercules was distracted by other girls. I was just so happy to be in his presence. But as we sit eating doughnuts and drinking coffee, women pass our window constantly, and he doesn't turn to glance at any of them. Boyles, my last boyfriend, couldn't focus on me for one whole minute before checking out all the females in the immediate area. And girls working behind the counter? Forget it. Boyles would flirt shamelessly—and sort of creepily —staring at them as if in a daze, needing to suck as much attention from them as he could absorb.

He had problems—that was for sure. Problems that Hercules doesn't seem to have. That's another reason why I feel so at ease with the man who has talked me into eating doughnuts before lunch.

"So, PG, how do you suggest we handle our friendship?" Hercules bites into a maple-frosted doughnut. It's the only one he insisted the girl put in the box.

I've just bitten into one with sprinkles. The sugary taste takes me by surprise.

"How is it?" he asks.

I realize I'm frowning, so I even out my expression. "Awfully sweet."

He chuckles. "Just like you."

I roll my eyes. "Such a flirt." I cock my head. "I propose that, as a friend, you don't flirt with me so much. Because…" My mouth is caught open. I can't say that it's because I'm having a hard enough time trying to resist him. "And touching me. You shouldn't do that either."

"What was that about, anyway?" he blurts.

I frown, confused. "What was what about?"

"Your lawyer being all handsy with you. You're his client. He shouldn't be touching you that way. He crossed a line."

I think I'm experiencing cognitive whiplash. *How did we get from me being supersensitive to his touch to Clive touching me? Plus…*

"Clive didn't touch me," I say.

Hercules jerks his head back so far that he might suffer actual whiplash. "What? He put his hand on your back."

"No, he didn't." I cock my head to the side, trying to remember. "Did he?"

"Yes, PG. He did."

Well, I'm certainly not going to negate what Hercules saw. He seems pretty rattled by it.

"Maybe he should recuse himself from representing you," he adds.

I lift my doughnut to my lips. "He doesn't have to because I'm never going back to that hearing room." I take a bite. "I think it's all stupid anyway. And I didn't know your family was seeking to share ownership in TRANSPOT."

Suddenly, Hercules tenses up. *Shoot, I'm mentioning our family business.* It's a red line, but I'm okay with crossing it.

Hercules leans forward, showing my favorite lopsided smile. "Well… we'll let our brothers fight it out, won't we?"

As if by power of suggestion, I nod. But I do like the sound of that. "Just so you know, I'm okay with what your family is asking for. I think my grandfather would be too." I shake my head as two faces come to mind. "I think all the tension and the pushback is coming from Max and Uncle Leo. My grandfather was a reasonable man. He was a saint." My own harsh tone catches me off guard. I compensate for it by forcing a smile. "He was."

Hercules's expression is unreadable. But I don't

think he agrees with me. I'm not sure why. He didn't know my grandfather.

His cellphone rings, and he casually puts his doughnut down, wipes his fingers, and takes his device out of his pants pocket. Watching him be so blasé about receiving a phone call is amusing, to say the least. I bet Hercules is the most cool-headed man in the world. I like that about him too.

He says hello, and his eyebrows ruffle as he looks at me. Then he rotates in his chair to point his body away from me. "Just get a grip," he says to whoever's on the other end of his phone. After listening some more, Hercules pinches the bridge of his nose. "Okay. Later."

After he ends the call, he sits still for a beat. And then he faces me with a manufactured smile.

"Everything okay?" I ask, concerned.

His face is tight. "That kiss has found its way to the wrong people. I just have to do a little damage control."

Suddenly I feel overwhelming dread. "Was that your brother Achilles?"

With a casual wink, he says that the caller was Achilles. Hercules is obviously trying to keep me from worrying. It's not working, though. I'm worrying. If our kiss found its way to Achilles, then soon Max, my dad, or even Leo will see it.

"Hey, PG," he abruptly says as he makes a phone call. It sounds like he's changing the subject. "I wanted to call you this morning, but I don't have your number. I should get it."

I'm about to tell him when he raises a finger to halt me. All the ease he had before his brother is back. I wait as he tells his driver where he is and how we'll be waiting for him.

"Unless you have your own car," he says, putting his phone back in his pocket.

*My own car?* "You mean like a hired driver?"

"Yes."

Shaking my head adamantly, I say, "No."

"Why not?"

"Because a cab or the subway works just fine."

"You're from one of the richest families in the world, and you ride around on the subway?"

I grimace, not quite understanding why he asked me that. Then I shrug and finish off my doughnut. "Sometimes I walk."

Hercules chuckles. "Oh, PG. What am I going to do with you? You're going to give me a heart attack, worrying about you."

I blurt a snort. "I do just fine."

He's watching me with a penetrating smile. "Are you ready?"

I press a hand against my fluttering stomach. "Yes."

Hercules's eyes are smoldering as he stands. I rise to my feet too. Once again, we're caught in an intense stare. *Gosh...* The level of attraction between us is nonsensical.

"Are you on your way to deal with the kiss?" I ask.

Nodding slowly, he says, "I am."

My eyebrows shoot up. "Well, Achilles has nothing to worry about since our kissing days are over. We're going to be just friends, right? Platonic friends?"

Hercules's chuckle sounds as if it escapes him. "Sure," he replies as he picks up the half-finished box of doughnuts. "Want to take these with you?"

I'm not sure he's looking to keep our relationship platonic, but I shake my head. "Too sweet."

He takes a step around the table to stand closer to me. His energy and presence are overpowering. The crotch of my panties is definitely soaked. He gets me so excited. I haven't had this much titillation down there since our New Year's Eve together.

"I guess I have to activate your sweet tooth, then." His voice is unabashedly seductive.

My breathing is heavy, and my chest rises high and falls low. Then a black SUV with dark tinted windows stops in front of the doughnut shop.

*An SUV? All that room in the back seat?*

I'm wearing a skirt. All Hercules has to do is unzip and insert. How easy it would be for him to be inside me yet again, filling me, pumping through me, pleasuring me...

*No way.* I need a break from him. I need space to think about whether I should spend more or less time with him.

I take a step back, putting a feeble amount of distance between us, and thumb over my shoulder. "I think... I mean, I'll just call a cab."

Hercules shakes his head. "No, you won't, PG. I'm not letting you leave me and take a cab. That's not happening."

I hold up a hand, palm out. "It's okay, Hercules. I've been taking cabs all my life. I'll be fine."

"It's not safe. How do you know the driver isn't a kidnapper?"

Shocked by his worry, I shake my head rapidly. "Kidnapper? Nobody's going to kidnap me."

I recall my cousin Treasure's fake kidnapping

during my junior year of high school. She was a freshman in college. I guess it's plausible that someone might get the idea to hold me for ransom. However, Treasure was not actually kidnapped—she was with a boy. And I'm certain that boy was Hercules's brother Orion. It seems I'm not the only Grove girl who can't resist the allure of a Lord boy.

He takes a step toward the door, gesturing with his head at the SUV. "PG, come on."

I shake my head adamantly. "I'll call Greg."

He frowns. "Who's Greg?"

"Our family's driver. He likes it when I contact him and ask him to take me somewhere."

Hercules's head falls back as his face crashes into the most severe frown. "Does he want you or something?"

"No!" I exclaim, shocked that he would think that. "He's known me since I was a little girl. He likes checking in. Seeing if I'm okay. And he always has words of advice. So if you're worried about my safety, I'll have Greg pick me up." I wave my hands to shoo him out of the doughnut shop before I lose my nerve and crawl into the back seat of his SUV and spread my legs for him. "So, you go. I'll be fine."

I gulp when he shows me my favorite lopsided smirk. "You want to get rid of me, PG?"

My eyes grow and then retract. I lick my lips, wondering if I should just say it. He's waiting for my response.

"It's just…" I heave a sigh. "We're working on a friendship, right?"

"Right…" There's a leading quality to his tone.

"Well, right now…" I can't believe I'm going to say this. I whisper, "Because right now, I don't feel so friendly toward you, if you know what I mean. And that's an SUV. And there's plenty of room for us to cross that line." My eyebrows flit up.

Hercules tosses his head back to grace me with a hearty laugh. *Gosh, I could listen to him do that all day long.*

He moves swiftly to close the distance between us. Then he wraps his arms around me. He's hard in several places—his chest, his arms, and certainly his cock.

"What's your number?" he says in my ear.

Through my tight throat, I tell him. Then he tells me his.

"It hasn't changed," I utter.

Hercules leans back to get a look at my face.

"You remember my phone number?" He looks totally amused.

*I'll never forget it.*

It's still in my contacts list. But I'll never tell him that. So I nod.

We're lost in each other's eyes. My lips crave a kiss. My tongue wants to taste his.

"Friends," he says breathlessly and then spies something over my head and out the window. Hercules says he'll call me later as he gusts to the exit. He points at me, standing in the doorway. "Don't forget to call Greg. Call him, PG."

"I will," I say, and I mean it.

Hercules nods and gives the extra doughnuts to a man who appears homeless. Then he reaches into his pocket, peels off bills from his money clip, and hands him cash too. He does that as if it is nothing to him, like he does it every day, all the time. The guy watches the SUV in awe as Hercules gets in and it peels away from the curb.

# Girl Talk

PAISLEY GROVE

I make it back to my office, and after my first two meetings, I sit at my desk, my face buried in my hands, trying to sort out the morning I had emotionally.

My intercom beeps, yanking me out of thoughts about my conversation with Greg. I check the time at the corner of my computer screen. It's almost four o'clock in the afternoon. I yawn. I'm exhausted, but I feel restless. And frankly, I really don't want to do any more work for the rest of the day.

I do not enjoy my job—not at all. Up until now, I would never have admitted that to myself or out loud. I miss coding. But I don't want to work for

Max or GIT. I want to work for myself. I want to go rogue.

"What's going on, Ru?" I say in a lackluster tone.

"You have a visitor."

"Did I miss an appointment on my calendar?"

"Nope. She's not scheduled to see you."

I rub my throbbing temple. I'm on the verge of telling Ru to send whoever it is away, but that wouldn't be wise. I'm the head of GIT's public relations and have to think about the company's image and the impression I give when people walk into our office. Basically, I can't be rude, cold, or indifferent. I must always be on my game, smiling, kind, and accommodating.

"Well, who is it?" I ask.

"She says it's a surprise," Ru replies.

I swivel in my chair to look out at my northern-facing city views. Pretty soon I'm going to be in my soaking tub. I can't wait.

"Could you please get a name?" I ask, doing a horrible job of constraining my agitation. Ru is usually a pro at managing random people who show up unannounced, seeking access to me.

Suddenly, my door flies open. "No, she cannot."

Recognizing the voice, I swivel around in my chair. "Treasure, what are you doing here?"

As usual, Treasure presents as a stunning beauty. She's wearing a pair of red, green, brown, and gold striped skinny pants with a fitted white T-shirt and brown leather espadrille sandals. Treasure's outfit is simple but chic and made especially for her.

"This is what I'm doing here," she says.

I notice the cellphone in her hand. She's closing the space between us, pointing the screen at me. It's a photo of Hercules and me sitting at a table for two inside the doughnut shop.

I gasp sharply as a knot forms in my chest. "What the hell?" *Who in the world is walking around town taking pictures of us?* It's weird. Scary.

Treasure plops down in the chair across from my desk and makes herself comfortable. "I saw the kiss too. So, you tell *me* what the hell is going on." Her eyes are shining which indicates that she's intrigued more than alarmed.

"It was nothing," I say, failing at playing it cool because I'm fidgeting in my seat.

Her head falls into a side tilt. "Pais. It's me. Number one, you can't bullshit a bullshitter. And number two, I can be accused of randomly kissing guys like Hercules Lord, but you can't. He means something to you."

I'm experiencing sensory overload, and knowing my cousin, I'm sure she's trying to get me to say something I can't take back. "Wait a minute," I say, throwing my hands up and waving them. Then I allow myself to feel the excitement of having my cousin surprise me with her presence. I mean, her bright eyes, bright-red mouth, and classically gorgeous face are right in front of me. "Treasure, what are you doing here? When did you get to New York?"

She wiggles her finger. "No. Don't change the subject. Are you screwing Hercules Lord again?"

"Again?" another familiar voice asks.

Treasure twists in her seat, and my eyes expand at the sight of Lake standing in the doorway.

*Damn it.* I cover my face with my hands and groan. *Great—now Lake knows.*

---

THE INTRODUCTIONS HAVE BEEN MADE. LAKE IS also a vision in a white cotton sundress with red embroidered flowers around the hem and a square neckline. She offsets the daintiness of her dress by wearing scuffed black combat boots. Treasure's eyes have rolled approvingly up and down Lake's form. Treasure's into people who are different and edgy. Lake is certainly both.

Ru had gone to the ladies' room which was how Lake so easily waltzed into my office. She said she peeped inside first and then heard us talking about Hercules. That was how she knew I wasn't in a business meeting.

I've been forced to explain how Hercules and I had sex years ago on New Year's Eve.

"Gosh, and you were a virgin?" Lake asks.

"Yes, she was." Treasure looks off, shaking her head. "There's something about those two," she muses as if I'm not sitting in front of her.

"If I knew they had that kind of history, I would've warned her by telling her that he'd being there," Lake says.

"Oh, no warning necessary. She knows to stay away from him. He's a Lord. Her parents would kill her."

Lake gasps like she's just seen a car crash. "Really? Like, literally kill her?"

Treasure shakes her head as a hard look sticks in her eyes. "No, not literally. But she'd wish she were dead."

One would have to know about her fling with Orion Lord to understand the sorrow in her voice.

I wave my hands vigorously. "Hello? I'm in the room."

Treasure and Lake look at me as if they're still lost in their thoughts.

"Okay, so Hercules and I talked this afternoon." I give them the bullet points about the arbitration hearing this morning, leaving out how I broke down at the end. "But we're not starting a romantic relationship at all." I won't tell them that we've decided to be friends.

Treasure watches me with a sly smile. "Don't lie to me, Pais. You can't lie to me. I know you too well."

My expression goes through multiple variations as I try to figure out what to change because Treasure is certainly reading my face. "He's engaged, Treasure," I blare, digging in and doubling down. "You know I respect the girl code. We both do."

Pressing her lips together, Treasure gives me a conciliatory nod. "True."

"But it's not a real engagement." Lake's eyes bulge as if she's questioning whether she should have revealed that.

"I know that already," I say to put her at ease. "Hercules told me as much."

Treasure grunts. "It doesn't change a thing. He always does what his mommy tells him to do. You see, it's not Achilles who's running the team—it's her. The father, Christopher, is long gone."

"That's right," Lake says, pointing at no one in particular. "He's somewhere tropical."

"Bermuda, Antigua, Barbados, Hawaii…" Treasure says.

I snort bitterly, shaking my head. I hate everything Treasure is saying about the Lords. "Yeah, but Hercules isn't…" My eyes widen. I almost went too far.

"You can say it." Treasure turns to Lake. "I used to bang Orion."

Lake rolls her eyes as though Treasure's revelation is no big deal. "Who hasn't?"

Treasure's neck juts forward. "Have you?"

"No, no, no, no," Lake says shaking her head adamantly. "But I used to work in the graphics department at LTI. That was where Mason and I met and fell in love." She pauses to let a blissful smile live on her lips for a few seconds. Then she sighs, indicating a mood change. "But Orion used to screw all the hottest females in the company."

"But you're hot," Treasure says.

"Thanks, but he knows he's not my type, and I'm not his. He likes more… designer types," Lake says. She and I examine Treasure.

Twisting under our scrutiny, Treasure blurts, "Why are you looking at me that way?"

Lake and I laugh.

Treasure shrugs jerkily. "You know what? Orion and I were a thing a long time ago. He's moved on. I've moved on. He's such an ass, though. He just screws around like I meant nothing to him." Treasure looks anguished as she closes her eyes, shakes her head, and whispers, "He's just an asshole."

Lake reaches out and rubs Treasure's back. I'm surprised my cousin is letting her do that. She never likes to be pitied or consoled. But I'm more shocked than anything that Orion is still able to make her cry. I can't wait to be alone with Treasure so we can fully explore her emotional reaction concerning Orion Lord. It may explain a lot about decisions she's made regarding other men.

"You know what? Men suck," Lake declares. "But for the record, Mason is the only man who doesn't."

Treasure and I laugh, thankful for the comic relief. Treasure snatches a tissue out of the box sitting at the corner of my desk. "On a lighter note, when are you getting married?"

Lake rubs her palms together and flexes her eyebrows at me. "That's why I'm here."

I eye her suspiciously. Anything having to do with ceremonies gives me the heebie-jeebies. Something about the order and rules makes traditional ceremonies feel like insurmountable tasks.

"Okay…" I say.

"My lead bridesmaid up and quit because Amy is too impossible for her to deal with, which I understand," she says, flipping a hand dismissively. "But you have thicker skin. But give me a while because I'm trying to figure out how to oust Amy and then ask you to be my maid of honor!"

I jerk my head back, feeling the sting of that little revelation. "No," I say, shaking my head. "Bridesmaid—okay, well, yes. But maid of honor, no."

"Deal." Lake gestures excitedly. "And don't worry about Hercules. You don't even have to look at him. I'll keep him far, far, far away from you."

"Hercules?" Treasure asks with an eyebrow raised curiously.

Lake sighs. "He's Mason's best man."

Treasure's watching me with a smirk. "Ooh. The plot thickens."

"Paisley, my office now," Max's voice booms through my office, making us all jump. He is standing in the doorway.

"Well, hello, Max," Treasure says, sneering at him.

He takes a moment to regard her. Max and Treasure never got along. He thinks she's a spoiled rabble-rouser who's been a bad influence on me. She thinks he's the mere definition of an asshole. However, he would do anything to protect her, and she knows it. And she would never throw him under the bus, and he knows it. In the end, family loyalty eclipses their dislike of each other.

"Treasure," he says in a dull voice. "Why are you in town?"

"Good to see you too." We both know she doesn't mean it. Treasure checks her expensive watch. "And whatever you have to say to Pais, make it quick. We have dinner reservations in fifteen."

I wrinkle my eyebrows, but he doesn't see it because he's checking his watch. But something's off about Max. The blood has drained from his face, and when he looks up, his eyes appear glazed over.

"What happened this morning at the hearing?" he asks.

"What hearing?" Treasure asks, grinning like she knows her question will annoy him.

Max stares daggers at her as his jaw tightens. His gaze shifts to Lake and stays on her for a fraction too long. Then his expression softens. *Oh, my God, he's attracted to her.*

Max is never attracted to anyone. Then I remember that Lake is an artist like Kiera, the one and only girlfriend Max has ever introduced me to. He has a type, apparently.

Treasure grins at Lake and then me. She too has probably noticed the effect Lake is having on my brother. Usually, Treasure would screw with him about it, but I think she's enjoying watching Max's discomfort.

"We'll talk in the morning." He spins on his heel and escapes my office so fast that he nearly leaves his shadow behind.

Once he's gone Lake, Treasure, and I look at each other with wide, smiling eyes before bursting out into laughter.

# Brother to Brother

HERCULES LORD

W hen I walk into Achilles's Upper East Side office on York Street, he and Orion are already engaged in conversation. Their talk halts when they see me. I'm familiar with that look on their faces. They've been talking about me.

"What are these videos that are circulating of you and the Grove daughter?" Achilles asks.

Closing my eyes, I sigh with dread. I have to think my way through this—or more like lie my way through it.

"It was nothing." I casually pad over to sit in on the black leather sofa against the wall. I stretch my arm across the back of the sofa, making myself comfortable. The trick to keeping my brothers off my ass is never letting them see me sweat.

"The hell it wasn't," Orion chimes in.

I narrow my eyes at him. He's doing a bad job of appearing as if seeing me kissing Paisley doesn't bring back memories of him and Treasure. Our mother didn't like it. She threatened to cut him off financially if he didn't break up with her and keep his distance. Orion was only eighteen then and relying on the family chest for a hefty monthly allowance. He lived rich and behaved rich. So the choice was simple—Treasure Grove had to go.

Achilles and my mother will probably threaten me in the same way. But it will only be a threat. I'm smarter than Orion. I have options. There's no way I'm going to be a slave to the Lord Trust for my entire life. There's no happiness in that—no freedom.

Achilles pounds his desk with a fist. "Cut the bullshit, Hercules."

I don't flinch. I stay as cool as a cucumber. "What do you want me to say?"

"Was that her red dress at your apartment?"

"No."

He snorts bitterly, aware that I'm lying. I don't care, though. *No* is my answer, and I'm sticking to it.

"You're marrying Lauren. We can't afford a fuckup."

My heart pounds. I can hear it in my ears. However, on the outside, I look unfazed. Although, whenever Lauren's name is mentioned, I get anxious. She makes me nervous. She wants to marry me. Sometimes she comments about the kids we'll have. She'll say something like, "We're distant enough cousins, aren't we? Our kids will be fine."

I can't imagine bringing life into the world with a woman I barely know and definitely do not love. When she asks me questions like that, I bite my tongue. She and I having children together is never going to happen.

"A statement is being published and sent twice to subscribers informing them that the video they saw had been doctored. *Rag Mag*, or whoever the hell they are, is going to back us up by apologizing for their mistake," Achilles says.

"It cost a lot of money to correct your fuckup," Orion adds, grinning.

I can tell he's liking watching me survive the pressure cooker. I rarely break, but on the rare occasions when I have broken, Orion has enjoyed it. He thinks I'm cocky, arrogant, and too smart for my own good. I think he's weak, entitled, narcissistic, and unserious. But the thing is, I'm right about him, and he's wrong about me.

Achilles dips his chin and glares at me with threatening eyes. "Stay away from her. Hear me?"

I rub my nose and sniff angrily. I'm not afraid of him. I see myself rising casually to my feet and telling him to go to hell before strolling out. But it's already occurred to me that I have to be the one to fix this shit because Achilles doesn't mind being beholden to that goddamn Lord Trust. The old man, our great-grandfather, must've been off his rocker when he put in place the complex web of twisting and turning hoops we have to jump through to get our hands on the money.

"Do you understand me?" Achilles growls, carefully enunciating each word.

*Bide your time.* I say, "I hear you."

And just like that, rage leaves Achilles's face, and the tightness dissolves from his shoulders. "You need to be seen out in public with Lauren more. In October, I'll have to argue before executors of the trust that your relationship is authentic. I need supporting evidence, not undermining shit like those videos." He takes a break with a sigh. "Starting tonight, I need you to go out with Lauren.

I made you dinner reservations." He waves me out of his office. "Now, go."

Smirking, Orion slouches in his chair. "By the way, it'll be a double date."

# A Double Surprise

PAISLEY GROVE

What a strange coincidence that Treasure was able to get us a table at The Chest of Chelsea. It wasn't until she mentioned it that I remembered Clive's lunch invitation. I really should call him and apologize for how I behaved at the hearing. He probably thinks I'm unstable.

The restaurant is a hotspot, the sort of place where people come with groups of friends to laugh, guzzle cocktails, and gorge on expensive food served in small portions. Our table is of interest to a lot of diners. People recognize Treasure Grove, and I'm not certain, but I think I'm being recognized too.

Lake and Treasure are getting on perfectly. It's no surprise that they like each other. Lake is unpretentious and isn't the competitive sort who has to suck all the attention toward herself. Treasure isn't that way, either, but she's always the first person anyone sees when we walk into a room. It can be pretty annoying for the kind of woman who needs the spotlight on her too. But I don't crave the attention, and neither does Lake. Plus, I love to see Treasure shine. She's charismatic and fun. It's easy for people to fall in love with her.

Lake is viewing Treasure as if looking at an interesting piece of art as Treasure orders just about everything on the menu and then asks if we want anything else.

"Did you really order all of that for yourself?" I ask.

Treasure hands her menu back to the waiter. "Nope. But since we're here, we might as well try everything."

I roll my eyes, yielding to Treasure's eccentric ways.

"By the way, Treasure," Lake asks as she hands her menu to the waiter. "I've been wanting to ask you something. And the need to know is killing me."

Treasure's expression is open. "To know what?"

Lake leans toward her and whispers, "Is it true you're engaged to Simon Linney?"

"Oh," Treasure says, looking off and playing coy. Then she tilts to be near Lake. It's like they're about to share a secret that I already know. "It's true."

"And you're not worried about his reputation?"

Treasure shrugs. "There's no doubt about it—he's a man whore, but he says he's reformed."

Lake hums and twists her Cupid's bow mouth thoughtfully.

Suddenly, Treasure thrusts herself toward Lake. "Oh no. Have you and he...?"

Lake shoots up two hands, showing Treasure her innocent palms. "No way. Never. But I know a few girls who've had relations with him. I heard he's good in bed but a prick out of bed."

Treasure nods as if she strongly agrees. "He's definitely an asshole. Maybe that's why I like him."

*Hmm...* I think.

"Or it could be his sultry English accent," Lake says. "It's like—butter."

"I think you might have a point, Treasure," I cut in.

Treasure's frowning at me like she's confused. "What point is that?"

"Your picker's lousy." I start counting them down finger by finger. "Jack, Corey, Mitch, Leon..."

So many faces come to mind that their names start to jumble. "Derek, Mich…"

"Maybe because I chase excitement, dear cousin, and you're dull."

*Ouch.* I straighten my back as my whole being absorbs Treasure's insult. Or maybe it wasn't an insult. I think it's the truth. I am dull. She's exciting. Her life is a hundred times livelier than mine. She has friends and lovers all around the world. And she would never agree to live in the Manhattan penthouse of her parents, Leo and Londyn. She has too many secrets to keep from them—fun ones. Up until reconnecting with Hercules, I've had no secrets.

"Well… Hercules Lord sure isn't boring," Lake says in my defense.

"But he's engaged," I whisper past the tightness in my throat.

Treasure reaches over and rubs my arm. "I'm sorry for saying that, Pais. Listen, I am dedicated to livening up your life. Remember, I made sure you had the best college roommate on the planet. Even when you were hell-bent on living in utter isolation with just you and your computer. And…"

I quickly put a hand on top of hers. "I forgive you." I need her to stop talking. Everything she's saying is too depressing. Maybe I should try to liven up my life. Maybe it's time.

Treasure smiles, flapping her eyebrows at me. "Thank you. And you're not dull."

I shake my head resolutely. "Oh, I'm dull."

"No, you're not," Lake chimes in.

I'm ready to change the topic of conversation.

"You're just going to have to move out of Xander and Heartly's penthouse, like, five minutes ago." Treasure leans in closer to me to whisper, "Especially if you're going to keep fucking Hercules Lord." She sits upright, smirking like she has me in checkmate. "I saw that kiss. The two of you had sex last night, didn't you?"

*Lie, Paisley.*

"Wait," Lake says with a start. "There's an apartment for sale in my building. It's not as luxurious as where you live now, but it's modern contemporary and has lots of bells and whistles because a Wall Street guy turned artist lives in it. But he's going back to Wall Street, and he's putting the apartment up for sale soon. I can get you in to see it before he puts it on the market."

"Ooh, we like the sound of that." Treasure raises her eyebrows as her gaze passes over me and then lands back on Lake. "Which building is it?"

Lake tells her.

Treasure jumps suddenly. "Oh my God. Do you know Davey Yee? Used to be a Wall Street guy but quit to become a sculptor."

Lake nods excitedly. "It's his…" She gasps. Her mouth stays stuck open as she stares at something behind Treasure. "Oh no."

Treasure and I turn to see what or who she's warning us about. I slowly fill my lungs with air as my head feels like it's detaching from my neck and floating like a helium balloon. *Oh no* is right. Hercules doesn't see me yet, but tonight he earns a ten out of ten in the looks department. He's wearing dark pants that fit his thighs like a glove. *So scrumptious…* His hair is combed neatly. I bet he's wearing that citrusy cologne that I love so much.

I push the air I've been holding out of my throat and finally expand my view to see Lauren with him. My shoulders cave in as my heart takes a beating.

"Orion?" Treasure winces.

As soon as she says that name, Hercules's panicked eyes lock on to mine. What was shaping up to be a great night of girl talk has just been flushed down the toilet.

# Just My Luck

HERCULES LORD

I can't look away from Paisley's angelic face. I can't stop tracking every change in her expression. She's not happy to see me with Lauren. I try to convey to her through my eyes that I can explain. But then the corners of her sexy mouth pull downward, and she cuts her eyes away from me and says something to Lake.

I squeeze my eyes shut and massage the bridge of my nose. *Damn it.* Of all the restaurants in New York City, Paisley has ended up in this one tonight.

"Well, well, well," Orion says, sneering at a woman who I think is Paisley's cousin Treasure. Tonight, he's with Clara, who's a knockout. But that's a given when it comes to Orion and the women he chooses to be seen with out in public.

"Could you put us next to some friends?" Orion asks the hostess.

"Oh…" The hostess says, rubbing the side of her face, staring at the reservation book in front of her as though she's in the throes of a crisis.

She knows that Orion Lord sits wherever he wants, whenever he wants. Achilles and I enjoy the same privilege in New York City. But we don't exploit it like Orion does.

The hostess looks up, a worried glint in her eye. The dining room is packed.

"We'll sit wherever you put us," I say to let the poor girl off the hook.

"The hell we will. I want to be near my friends, right over there," Orion says loudly, pointing at Paisley's table, where two waiters are setting several plates in front of them. *Why so much damn food?*

The hope on the hostess's face fades to despair.

"Is that Lake with that girl Paisley Grove?" Lauren drapes herself around my arm.

I can't free myself from Lauren's death grip without causing another scene. Also, I'm distracted by Treasure Grove, who's approaching us. She resembles Paisley with her long, shapely legs and perfectly placed facial features. It's like she's walking on a runway as she closes the distance between us.

Her shoulders are back and her chin up. She knows people are watching, and she's giving them a show.

My gaze flicks back to Paisley, who's observing me just as I had her. My heart pounds hard and loud. I can feel it pulsing in my ears.

"Well, hello, beautiful," Orion says without regard to his date's feelings.

"Why are you making a scene?" Treasure purrs.

"You're still doing that, huh?"

"Doing what?"

"Ordering enough food to feed an army. How about you let us join you? Clara here wouldn't mind, would you?"

I'm only able to look away from Paisley after Clara says, "Whatever."

I'm shocked that Clara hasn't figured out what's going on here. Orion is openly flirting with and pursuing Treasure Grove. On the ride over, Clara and Orion were sucking face like no one was watching. I know for a fact that whatever's going on between them won't last, but until now, they were pretending to be a real couple.

But although his date's instincts are off, my date's are on. Holding my arm tightly, Lauren is getting territorial. I swallow hard, unable to look away from Paisley. *Damn, she's sexy.* I recall her face while I was pumping in and out of her. The expression she held as I gave it to her. So damn sexy.

"Hi, Hercules," Treasure says.

I rip my gaze off Paisley. "Hi," I barely say and then clear my throat. "Don't worry. We're sitting at our own table."

Orion points his hand at a table not that far from where Paisley and Lake are whispering to each other. I wish I knew what they were saying. "One just became available," he says as a group of patrons rise out of their chairs.

Treasure casually grabs the edge of the hostess desk and smiles at the girl behind it.

"Lena, please show these hot and strapping Lord brothers and their beautiful dates to a table far, far, fucking far away from mine. And don't worry about this one"—she thumbs at Orion—"throwing a tantrum. He can't fire you. I won't let it happen."

Before I can register what's happening, Orion takes a step to stand behind Treasure. Everyone, including me, can see him pushing his cock against her. He whispers something in her ear.

Treasure snorts and shakes her head. "You never change, do you?" Then, like a streak of lightning, she spins around and slaps him.

Gasps erupt, and the chatter turns a few decibels quieter.

"No. I will not be doing that with you ever again. And I own this place. So, as I said, your table will be far, far, far away from mine, or frankly, you can eat somewhere else." With that said, Treasure rakes her fingers through both sides of her hair and then glares at me. "Leave my cousin alone."

I'm uneasy as I watch her stroll confidently back to her table.

"Everybody's dinner is on me tonight," Orion announces.

Treasure stops in her tracks and whips around to stare at him like she wants to wring his neck. Snickering, Orion wraps an arm around Clara's waist and winks at her. I shoot a look over at Paisley, taking her temperature, trying to figure out if her expression will tell me what she thinks about how the scene between her cousin and my brother is playing out. But either she's unreadable, or my inner turmoil isn't allowing me to see what I'm looking for.

"WE HAVEN'T DISCUSSED OUR HONEYMOON YET," Lauren says to Clara, who asked if we made any plans yet.

"Try any resort along the Indian Ocean. A client… somebody took me to a resort along that ocean. It was nice. That's all."

"Maybe we should look into it," Lauren replies. I think she's talking to me.

"Hey," Orion barks, snapping his fingers in front of my nose.

I flinch, blinking myself out of the trance that staring at Paisley has put me in. She hasn't looked at me since we were seated across the restaurant and far from their table. Orion doesn't have a line of sight on Treasure, but fortunately, I have one on Paisley. She's tight. I think she's fighting the urge to turn in my direction. I keep willing her to do it.

"What the hell," I growl, glaring at Orion. In my peripheral vision, I see Paisley stand up and walk away from her table. "I'll be back."

I hop to my feet and follow her to wherever she's going.

# Nipping at My Heels

PAISLEY GROVE

Weaving through the tables, I glance over my left shoulder. Treasure was right—Hercules is following me. She said he would, and he is.

"He's staring at you like you're his lost puppy and Mommy says he can't have you back," Treasure said. We discussed this scenario beforehand, and Treasure gave me instructions. "Get up and go to the private bathrooms. He'll follow you, and when you get him alone, tell him to knock it off because people are starting to notice." She then passed me a keycard to the VIP lounge and bathroom and pointed me in the direction I should go.

I enter a dimly lit hallway with blue lights. Hercules catches the door before it closes.

"Paisley," he calls.

My heart is stomping beats as his voice sends a giddy thrill through me. Maybe being alone with him in such a sexy atmosphere wasn't a good idea. Plus, there's more nagging at me than Hercules being here with Lauren. My cousin is not the sort who throws empty insults to win a spat. When she referred to me as dull, she meant it.

But then Lake said Hercules was exciting. I never knew that about him. I've known him for the longest amount of time, but she has had more quality time with him since her fiancé is his best friend.

His footfalls speed up. I slow down to let him catch up to me. When he's close enough, I turn around, and we're standing face-to-face.

"Hey," he whispers and then swallows audibly.

"You didn't tell me you were going to dinner with your fiancée this morning." My tone is harsher than I want it to be. Maybe a dull person cares about hurting other people's feelings even when they deserve it.

"The date wasn't my call. I'm just doing my duty, PG. You know that. We talked about it."

My face collapses into a severe frown. "When did we talk about you going on a double date with your fiancée, your brother, and…?" I recall what Treasure said about Orion's date. She accused her of being a high-class prostitute. "Is Orion's date a call girl?"

Staring into Hercules's confused eyes, I'm wondering why I asked that. Maybe I need Treasure to be wrong. If she's wrong about Orion's date, then she might be wrong about me being dull too.

"Yes," Hercules bluntly replies.

*Damn it.* His answer hits me like a wall of wind. His brother's out with a prostitute, and he's with his fake fiancée. There's something grossly wrong about that.

I shake my head. "You know what? I don't want to be your friend. Just leave me alone."

His strong hands clamp down on my waist before I'm able to walk away. "Paisley, come on— we talked about this. I told you my family is making me marry her for the money. But I'm trying to figure a way out of it."

"Well, it doesn't look like it to me," I say, unable to get the two of them out of my head. Hercules and Lauren are aesthetically the perfect couple. Now that I think about it, they resemble each other, and that could be because they're related. *Gross.*

Hercules's eyes chase mine until I'm looking at

him again. I want to turn away from him, but I can't. His hands hold me tighter, and he tips back as he draws me closer, never losing sight of my face.

"I don't want you to stop being my friend, PG. We're supposed to get to know each other better, remember? Don't you want more doughnuts?" He cracks a tiny smile. "I'll get you more doughnuts."

Oh God, I want to kiss him so badly. But all I can think about is him and Lauren. "Am I dull?" The words just sort of fall out of my mouth on their own.

He's frowning sympathetically. "No. Why did you ask me that?"

Closing my eyes, I shake my head. I don't want to repeat what Treasure said about me. Maybe he'll believe it. After all, she knows me better than he does.

"Paisley." There's need in the way he whispers my name.

My inhalations are deep, and exhalations spread wide across his face. I feel as if I'm falling apart. *Who could have guessed my day would start with that arbitration hearing and end with Hercules and me alone in a hallway of the restaurant that my cousin has revealed she owns?* One thing is for sure—unlike me, Treasure is full of surprises.

"Open your eyes," Hercules says.

I can feel his mouth nearer to mine. I think maybe I should start being full of surprises too. Maybe I'll start with a forbidden kiss.

A soft but piercing beep reverberates through the hallway. Hercules and I take a quick step away from each other. The door opens, and a woman in a revealing black dress that fits her body like a glove glances at me before keeping her eyes posted on Hercules. Her walk has turned slinkier, more seductive. I'm not surprised. He's just the sort of man who inspires that kind of response from the opposite sex.

Hercules is frowning at her as if he is put off that she's disturbed our privacy. I take advantage of the moment to break out of his hold and rush to the door.

The last thing I hear him say is "PG."

But I don't turn around to look at him again. I've freed myself from the sexual magnetism that exists between us, at least for now.

# A Night to Remember

PAISLEY GROVE

We tried to carry on with dinner for as long as we could. We were girls who were determined to not let a pair of boys ruin our night, but Lake received a phone call from Mason. As soon as she hung up, she seemed distracted. And I think Orion and his pay-to-play date got to Treasure more than she let on. Of course, having a view of Hercules and Lauren irked me. So we had all the leftovers boxed up, split the food between us, and left.

When I got home, I showered and then cleansed and moisturized my face. Now I'm in bed, wearing panties and a tank top. I'm sitting against the bed's large gray headboard, scarfing down a fancy sort of cracked lamb Bolognese from Treasure's restaurant. The portion is very small, the size of an appetizer. Regardless, the food hits the spot. It's really tasty, and my stomach isn't growling anymore. So, those are pluses.

I gaze at a scene from tonight's news playing on the oversized TV that slides out of the foot of my bed. But I'm not really paying attention to what's being said or shown, although I can tell the content is very sensational.

I shake my foot, fighting the urge to call Hercules. I'm surprised he hasn't reached out to me. Maybe Orion talked some sense into him. Although if Orion is the kind of person Treasure says he is, then he's not one who talks much sense into anybody.

The back of my head collapses against the headboard as my sigh mirrors a deflating balloon. *Who are we kidding, anyway?* A friendship with Hercules is like trying to eat one potato chip without my mouth watering for the next, and the next, and so on. The sex we had last night was nothing short of epic. My body is still reeling from his hands all over my skin, and him being inside of and on top of me. We almost kissed tonight.

I shake my head just as my cellphone chimes. Like a frightened cat, I leap out of bed and pounce on my purse sitting on the oversized armchair. My heart constricts when I read the name on the screen.

On the third ring, I take a breath, get a grip, slide the answer bar to the left, and calmly say, "Hello."

---

THIS IS RECKLESS OF ME—OF US. HERCULES ASKED if I wanted to do something that wasn't dull.

Chuckling, I crooned, "What do you have in mind?"

"You'll have to wait and see," he said, flirting.

Ultimately, I agreed to spend time with him. Hercules ordered a car to pick me up and take me to a building in our neighborhood. I was given access to a private elevator, which raced me to the rooftop floor. On a helipad, Hercules and a helicopter were waiting for me.

And now we're soaring through the sky. We have earphones on so we can hear each other over the purring engine. I can't help but split my attention between Hercules and the lights twinkling below us. Gosh, New York is a gorgeous state. The whole East Coast can be majestic. California always felt new and bold, but this side of the country feels like history.

"How are you?" Hercules asks.

I rip my gaze from the landscape below and smile at him. "Where are you taking me?"

His mouthwatering smile grows wider. "You can't handle surprises, PG?"

"Yes. I can handle surprises." I'm giddy, beaming like I would have been if Hercules asked me out on a proper date back in high school.

His toothy grin takes my breath away. Gosh, his teeth are so white. He takes care of himself. That's a turn-on too. Then he says how surprised he was to learn that Treasure owned the Chest of Chelsea.

"So was I." I gnaw on my bottom lip thoughtfully. "I don't think her parents know."

Hercules seems to consider what I've just said. I'm waiting for him to say something that'll lead me to say more. But he's taking too long, and I want to say what I've been thinking about the whole mess of Treasure buying a restaurant and being engaged to a legendary fuckboy actor too.

"Because if they knew, her dad would've

mentioned it to his wife, and his wife would've bragged to my mom about how regardless of being cut off from our grandfather's trust, Treasure, like me, was out in the world making it on her own. And probably even more successful since she wasn't at all connected to the family billions. And then my mom would've called me to discuss how Treasure knows nothing about owning a restaurant." Shaking my head while gazing at Hercules unfocused. "I can hear my mom ask, 'How many restaurants survive their first year? One in three or one in four?'" I say, mimicking her Southern Californian accent. "She wouldn't wait for me to get her the accurate answer before declaring that Treasure would definitely be on the losing side of that statistic." I sharpen my focus on Hercules.

He looks troubled. "Your family sounds like my family."

My sigh is suffused with heaviness. "Well, at least Treasure and I have made a pact to never engage our mothers in negative speech about each other."

"That's very progressive of the both of you."

His compliment makes me smile. "Thanks."

He smiles again, setting his fiery focus on my mouth. I think he wants to kiss me. But we can't kiss. Regardless, I go on to explain how my mom and Treasure's mom are competitive. There's history between Treasure's mom and my mother who used to be a world-class fashion model, and Leo—Treasure's father—and Xander, my dad.

"Whenever we're together, my parents do this odd duo act where they tell the story of how Heartly Rose chose Xander over Leo. And that sort of explains why people say Treasure and I look alike. Because the Grove brothers have similar taste." I roll my eyes at how amusing and crazy that all sounds. Sometimes I have to remind myself that the "grown-ups" in my universe are not gods. They're merely human beings with pasts that contain elements of tragedy or comedy, depending on how I look at it.

Hercules watches me with the same penetrating gaze and sexy smile he held before I decided to turn into a motormouth.

"Sorry, I'm talking too much. I had a glass of wine tonight," I say with a sigh, although I don't think that's the reason why I feel so uninhibited. It's him. He makes me so comfortable that it's hard to be my same guarded self when I'm around him.

"No, please talk. I love watching you talk."

I swallow the extra moisture that's poured into

my mouth. Hercules is watching me. And I'm not dimwitted. I comprehend the meaning behind the eyes he's giving me. But I can't succumb to Hercules's powers of seduction.

I quickly look out the window. The earth is dark with only spatters of light. We're far away from the city. I have a comment to make about where we might be going, but I'm afraid that if I speak to him or look at him, he'll soon end up inside me.

*Get a grip, Paisley. We're just friends—right?*

"Your cousin and my brother have a real problem with each other," Hercules says.

I'm guessing he's trying to keep me talking. I brace myself before looking into his intense eyes and at his perfectly handsome face. I'm seeing him again. Gosh, he's gorgeous. In my mind's eye, I see him on top of me, sliding in and out of me. That look of overwhelming enjoyment on his face as he makes love to me. I want that again. I want that right now. My heart knocks in tune with the sound of the engine.

"She's a real spitfire," I finally say.

"That's why Orion likes her. She's hard to pin down. He likes his women that way. Because he's hard to pin down."

I snort a chuckle. "That makes sense."

"You're hard to pin down too," Hercules says.

For a moment I consider what he claims. I come up with no reason why he would think that. "Me?"

"Yeah, you." His flirtatious smirk is the star of his face.

*Oh my God—yummy.*

"Why do you say that?" I'm barely able to force the words through my tight throat.

"You've always made it hard for a guy to get to know you better."

"What?" I shake my head vigorously. "That's not true. And believe me when I say that not many guys wanted to get to know me. I'm not the type. And I'm okay with that."

Hercules relaxes more in his seat. "You said it yourself. You resemble Treasure Grove and your mom. They're both knockouts, just like you."

My simpering gaze falls to my lap as I picture my face and then Treasures. We definitely resemble each other. But there's something inherently different about us.

"You don't believe me?" he asks just as the pilot announces that we're descending.

Suddenly, I have a little more insight into the whole notion of my looks. "I don't think I allowed myself to care too much about how attractive I am to the opposite sex. I've been too busy parent-pleasing and trying to live up to this huge legacy my grandfather left behind."

He grunts as though I've piqued his interest. "What happened at the end of the hearing today?"

My eyes grow wide as my mind experiences a traffic jam of thoughts.

"I don't know," I whisper. Actually, I think I do know why I suffered a meltdown. But the explanation is very complicated and the source of a lot of pain I've been keeping to myself for a long time.

"Does it have something to do with your grandfather?" he asks.

*Say it, Paisley.*

But then the pilot announces that we're landing and instructs us to keep our heads low as we exit the helicopter. Hercules is still watching me as if he's reading every thought I might be having. I keep my eyes away from him. I wonder if I'm ready to tell him what I found six years ago after digging through my grandfather's secrets. He would be the first person I'd ever tell.

When I gather the nerve to look at him again, Hercules is regarding me with worry and attraction. But gosh. I can still hardly believe I'm riding in a helicopter with the person I've had a crush on for almost half my life.

Now, he's all smiles, and so am I. Our longing for each other can't be denied. Wherever Hercules is taking me, keeping the theoretical chastity belt locked is going to be my biggest worry.

# Skinny-Dipping

### HERCULES LORD

"Nobody will find us out here," I say to PG as we enter my Bridgehampton estate.

I walk inside, but Paisley's feet remain glued to the porch. "Are you planning on having sex with me? Because that's not what friends do," she says.

It's hard to look at her soft pouty lips and wide cautious eyes without growing a boner. My cock is firm, but there's nothing I can do about that. It wants what it wants, and it wants Paisley Grove. The helicopter ride was a storm of sexual tension, at least for me. I couldn't look at her with trying to tamp down my desire for her. I'm still trying to figure out why she has this effect on me. Yes, I hope to make love to her before our time wraps up. I won't be overt about it. I'll never force her to do anything she's not ready to do. But damn—I hope she's ready.

"What happens will happen," I say.

PG crosses her arms loosely over her plump breasts covering her knotted nipples. "But nothing's going to happen."

She's excited. That's a good sign. But I shrug like I don't notice that she wants me too. "It's all on you, PG. Wherever you lead, I'll follow."

Her expression asks me to please not cross the line with her tonight. Don't seduce her. Keep my distance. As though she's able to read my mind, I nod, assuring her I'll try not to.

Her nod mimics mine, and then she cautiously steps over the threshold. Her nearness drives me crazy. Her scent...

"What is that?" I ask.

She folds her arms tighter, appearing even more nervous. "What's what?"

"That perfume you're wearing."

"Oh," she says and tells me.

"It's nice."

"Thanks."

"Are you ready to wash it off?" I ask. I'm proud of myself for what I have in mind for us tonight.

"Huh?" PG's utterly confused expression is so damn sexy. Everything this woman does is sexy. I'm glad she walked back into my life last night. But I'm unaccustomed to feeling the kind of power she has over me.

I gulp and make my breaths even. "Come with me, and I'll show you what I'm talking about."

---

THE LAST THING OFF IS MY UNDERWEAR. PAISLEY gasps, staring at my boner like it's coming to gobble her up.

"That can't be helped," I explain, grinning and pointing two fingers at my cock.

I'm naked, thinking I'd better jump into the pool—which I warmed remotely two hours ago—before she faints. She is more sheltered than any other woman I've been with which is odd because she has enough money to go anywhere in the world and do anything she likes. Her parents must really have a strong grasp on her. I've learned that type of grip is more mental than physical.

To put her out of her misery, I dive into the

water, eager for her to join me. But PG is still fully dressed.

"Come on in," I say after I rise to the surface. "The water feels good. It's warm."

PG raises a hand in objection. "Wait. You want me to strip out of my clothes and swim naked in a swimming pool with you and your... Erection?"

Tired of her stalling, I playfully splash her with water. "Get in. I promise I'll keep him away from you."

She giggles as she twists her sexy body to avoid being sprayed by water.

I swallow, imagining her naked through her oversized faded jeans and V-neck T-shirt that lies over her scrumptious breasts. It's cute how she groans and hugs herself. She wants to do it—I can tell.

"The water feels good. And we've had a long day. Let your hair down. Relax. There's nothing dull about skinny-dipping, baby."

A look passes over her face. The word *dull* could have been triggering for her. I'm about to apologize for saying it when she snatches her shirt off.

*Holy shit.* Her beautifully formed breasts are cradled by a red lace bra. I've noticed something about PG.

"You like sexy underwear?" I ask before she drops her jeans, and I'm dumbfounded by her hips and crotch in her matching panties.

It takes a beat to register that her neck is bent, and she's assessing herself like she doesn't know what I'm talking about. Then Paisley steps to the lip of the swimming pool and raises her arms, aiming her fingers, preparing to dive in.

"Whoa, whoa, whoa," I say.

She freezes, and her eyebrows raise. "What?"

I grin, loving that she's playing coy. "You know what. I'm naked. That means you have to get naked too."

Screwing her mouth squeamishly, Paisley drops her arms to her sides. "Do you really think that's a good idea?"

"Yep," I reply, feeling strongly about how good the idea truly is.

She snickers. "No hesitation on your part."

I laugh as I push a pillow of water at her. "PG, stop stalling."

She giggles as she twists away from me.

"Plus, you're just as tempting in your sexy panties and bra."

She gives herself another once-over, again

appearing as if she has no idea what I'm talking about. "This is sexy?" she finally asks.

I can't stop grinning. I've always been turned on by that trait of hers. She's damn clueless about her sex appeal. PG is a solid ten out of ten without even trying.

*Friends, Hercules.*

I fight the urge to tell her what I want to do to her while she's wearing those panties. I want my tongue over her clit through the red lace as she wriggles against my mouth. And when she releases a shivering moan as she comes, I'll snatch her panties off, slam my absurdly hard cock inside of her, and pump until I blast off.

I throw my hands up out of impatience. "PG!"

"Okay, here goes nothing," she says.

Her panties are off. My breaths shudder as she pulls the straps of her bra down her shoulders and slides the band from the back to the front to unclip it. The entire show of her taking off her bra is nearly more than I can stand. I wish I hadn't watched it all.

To get a grip on my excitement, I look away from her to focus on the cabanas. I've been meaning to change them out. Maybe skinny-dipping in the Hamptons wasn't such a good idea.

Then she dives in, splitting the water beside me. Paisley's a good swimmer. Her strokes are long and graceful. I want to keep watching her, but I force myself to look away and think about something else. It's already after midnight which means it's Saturday morning. I'm supposed to meet with Mason in my office at nine. He's supposed to read me a list of products we can push to the market fast. Recalling how we hardly made a profit last month and how we're barely getting by this month eases my arousal.

"The water does feel good," Paisley says, holding on to the edge of the swimming pool.

I swim to her. We're face-to-face. Water glistens her soft skin. Her face is lit up like the moon. I'm making her happy tonight, and there's no better feeling in the world than knowing I've done that.

"I warmed it up just for you," I tell her.

She rewards me with an appreciative smile as her eyes drop bashfully from my face to the shimmering blue liquid. I should kiss her. *Just do it.*

But it's not what she wants. She doesn't even know Lauren, yet she wants to respect her. I love that about PG too. I'm certain if the roles were reversed, Lauren wouldn't show her the same courtesy.

"You've never swum naked, I presume," I say in a feeble attempt to talk about something, anything.

"Never," she replies, beaming. "It's not like I didn't have a chance. It just never occurred to me to do it. But..." She closes her eyes and tilts her head back. "This feels good."

I spread myself in front of her. Her soft body stiffens against mine. I can do this—feel her without wanting to fuck her.

"You want to play?" I ask

"Play?" she asks in a high-pitched, worried voice.

Her lips are wet, tantalizing. I refocus on her eyes to stop myself from kissing her. "Yeah, play."

"How do you mean?"

"Want me to show you?"

PG tapers an eye. "Does it involve sex?"

I laugh, shaking my head. "Unfortunately for me, it doesn't."

She simpers bashfully, her gaze admiring the water. "Okay, then. What the hell. Let's play."

"Brace yourself," I say, grinning. Then I quickly take her by the waist and use all my strength to toss her up.

Paisley laughs as she balls up, pinches her nose, and drops into the water. She rises to the surface and does the backstroke to the other side of the pool. Her tits poke above the water.

My hands ache to touch her, and my tongue needs to taste her. But I take a deep breath and count to ten as I look away from temptation.

*Shit… This is going to be a long night.*

# Temptation

## PAISLEY

**E**very time Hercules puts his hands on me and throws me, my sex tingles. His cock likes to dangle between my thighs when he's close. It's clear that we both know we're playing with fire. If we choose to go further, all he has to do is slide himself inside me and give me what I so desperately crave.

We've done laps together and swum around each other. Now I'm clinging to the wall, and he's in front of me, gazing into my eyes as we compare the places in the city that we both frequent. We never visit the same places, and his list is a lot longer than mine. But we do note some possible near misses.

My eyelids turn heavy as I yawn. "I guess I don't get out much."

"Getting sleepy?" he asks.

I nod as I look up. The sky is turning light purple. Soon, the sun will appear on the horizon.

"I've had a great time playing with you, PG," he whispers.

The lust in his eyes can't be ignored. Our breath spreads over each other's faces. When he moves in closer, I can feel how hard he is. We can do it, and no one will ever know. I'm tempted.

"What are you doing tonight?" Hercules asks.

"Tonight?" I say breathlessly.

"It's past midnight. Yesterday is officially over."

"Oh…" I chuckle.

His moist lips stretch into a delicious smirk. "Aren't we hanging out, becoming better friends?"

*Oh, he's so bad.* His cock floats up and nudges my hood. "Mm-hm," I say. My body sizzles as I try to control my insatiable need to let him inside me.

"Then…" Fortunately, Hercules pushes away from me and treads water in the middle of the swimming pool. "We'll do something tonight. Somewhere no one can see us." He frowns. "What's it called? *Mag Rag.*"

I laugh. It's cute how he bungles their name. "It's *Top Rag Mag.*"

"Right. We'll stay away from those assholes."

"Out of sight, out of mind?" I ask, grinning.

Hercules looks as if he's about to say something, but then he's quiet. "Out of sight, out of mind," he finally says.

———

WE DRY OFF, TAKING SNEAK PEEKS AT EACH OTHER as we put our clothes back on. Then we sit next to each other on the helicopter ride back to the city. When we touch down on the same helipad we lifted off from, Hercules gently shakes me awake. I slowly open my gritty, heavy eyelids. Gosh, I'm so tired. I realize my face is against his strong chest and his arm is around me. My eyes pop open, and I sit up.

But there's no drawing me away from his allure as we gaze into each other's eyes. He gently strokes my cheek with the back of his hand. My vulnerable heart is thumping like a piston.

"See you tonight," he says. He's not asking because he doesn't have to.

I nod. "See you tonight."

———

"ARE YOU BORED?" LAKE ASKS.

And right on cue, I yawn again. It's like I can't stop doing it. I'm so exhausted that I can hardly keep my eyes open. Once I got home last night, I stripped off my clothes, washed the chlorine out of my skin and hair, dried off, moisturized, got into bed naked, and grabbed Mr. Man from my bedside drawer. I had to get rid of the excitement in my nether regions. Hercules had made me so horny that I couldn't stand it.

Then I fell asleep. I hadn't been dreaming for too long before my cellphone chimed and woke me up. It was Lake.

"I have a treat for you," she sang as if she'd woken up well-rested and ready to conquer the city.

I squinted at the time on the screen. It was 9:33 on Saturday morning. I was usually up two hours before then.

"What treat?" I muttered, rubbing my left eye.

"Get over here and let me show you!"

She didn't have to twist my arm. I liked being friends with Lake because she was never boring. I figured if she had a surprise for me, it was something I wanted to experience. So I told her I'd be over soon and then suited up in running pants and a lightweight tank top and tied my athletic jacket around my waist. I hadn't gone for a run since

Thursday morning. It was now Saturday. I was due for a good run through the park to Chelsea where Lake lived.

The surprise is that I have been granted an exclusive tour and a first crack at an off-market apartment in Lake's building, the one she mentioned at dinner last night. Apparently, when she told Davey Yee that she had a friend who might be interested in his place and then gave him my name, he knew exactly who I was and asked how fast I could close.

"Fast," Lake said. "Very fast."

So now I'm in Davey Yee's abandoned apartment. Well, the furniture is still present, but he's already moved back to Lower Manhattan. Lake's last question regarding my being bored still hangs in the air.

I stifle another yawn. "How could I be bored? Look at this place."

We've toured every inch of the clean eighth-floor flat which is the unit that owns the rooftop deck. Davey has done a lot of work up there. A retractable glass ceiling covers the entire space. He certainly spent a lot of money to have that done. A self-cleaning mode is built into the system too. It's all pretty cool. And Davey has the Rolls-Royce of barbecue pits.

Expensive patio furniture surrounds an oblong glass and steel fire pit. An eighty-inch television screen automatically slides out of a block-of-wood base. But there's a lot more—an aboveground spa large enough to seat twenty people and a fully equipped exercise room with its own TV and surround-sound system. And potted flowers, trees, and bushes are tastefully positioned throughout. The space really does look and feel like my own urban oasis.

The broker is Van Calloway, an overly well-groomed man in a shiny gray suit. Whenever he can tell I like something about the apartment, he flashes a huckster's white-tooth grin, raises his tweezed eyebrows, and says, "Nice, huh?"

"As you know, the only offer is asking price." He's still displaying that smile.

I raise an eyebrow, wondering whether he knows he's speaking to Xander Grove's daughter.

Lake grasps me by the wrist. "Is that going to be a problem?" she asks me. "The asking price is awfully high. I can talk to Davey, though. He still owes me."

Instead of asking her "Owes you for what?" I yawn again.

"What is up with you?" she asks.

I shake my head. "Nothing. I just couldn't sleep last night."

"Oh," She rubs my back sympathetically. "Was it hard seeing-you-know-who at The Chest last night?"

I fail at stopping myself from looking stupefied by her question. I really don't want to outright lie to my friend. It takes me several seconds to realize that the truth will suffice. "Yeah, it was hard."

"Aww... well, let's hope you get some rest after we're done," Van says, redirecting our attention back to him. His tone indicates that he doesn't know who we're talking about, nor does he care to know. I think he wants me to make a decision so he can move on with his day.

"Seven point five million cash," I say. "And we can close in seventy-two hours."

Van laughs with no humor. "The asking price is nine million, nine hundred ninety-nine thousand, nine hundred ninety-nine."

I want to blurt a laugh at that ridiculous price, but I keep my wits about me. "All cash, add the furniture, no inspections, four-day close, and I'll give you seven million."

"Except the bed," Lake says, finger raised.

"Actually, all the beds." She shakes her head at me. "I promise you, Paisley, you don't want them."

---

DAVEY COUNTERS WITH EIGHT MILLION, WHICH I thought he would, and I accept. I call Corina Correa, my personal financial advisor, who has no ties to the family bank. She'll handle the sale on my behalf.

After the deal is made, I'm too anxious to go home and sleep for a few more hours. Instead, I go upstairs to Lake's place, and she makes pancakes and scrambled eggs for us. She reveals that when her fiancé called during dinner, he said that he had passed out again. He was walking to the bathroom, and the next thing he knew, he was coming to on the floor in the hallway. He suspects he hit the wall first, and that broke his fall.

"He could've hit his head and died. And I wouldn't have even been there for him." Lake's shoulders have collapsed, and she looks so worried.

"You said it happened 'again.' Has Mason fainted before?"

She nods softly. "We think he's just overworked. LTI isn't doing so well financially. Their new products keep flopping. Mason has no idea what to do about it. It's stressing him out."

"Oh," I say, frowning sympathetically. I wonder why Hercules hasn't mentioned his company's woes to me.

"I've been trying to talk Mason into finding another job, but he doesn't want to leave Hercules. He treats him well. Hercules treats all his employees well." She grimaces then looks off thoughtfully. "Speaking of Hercules, what's really going on between the two of you?"

I'm on the verge of asking if Mason has gone to the doctor yet, but that question fades from the tip of my tongue. "Huh?"

"*Top Rag Mag* wrote another story about you two. See…"

She gets her cellphone and shows me a post with a photo of me at the restaurant last night with a forlorn look on my face. A similar photo of Hercules is next to mine. They're comparing our reactions to each other. I don't even want to read the caption, but I can't help myself.

*Sources say this is how they looked at each other through dinner. Then he followed her into a private hallway. We wonder what happened in secret. More of this?*

Beneath is a repeat video clip of our Thursday-night kiss.

I close my eyes as I sigh, wishing I hadn't seen that. I hand Lake her phone. "Are they stalking us?"

"Well… yeah," she says, to my surprise. "But it's easy to write this kind of story when you both behave as if you're in love with each other. Are you?"

Suddenly, I'm warm, and I remember that I'm wearing a jacket. I take it off.

"He's getting married, Paisley." She raises a hand as if I were going to say something to negate that. I wasn't. "And I know he's being forced into it. And Hercules doesn't strike me as the type who can't live without his sleek penthouse and fancy car and driver and billionaire lifestyle. But if he's going to keep LTI operational, then he needs to marry Lauren. The company needs the money. At least, that's what Mason says."

I cough to clear the frog out of my tight throat and say, "Hercules and I are just friends." I'm shocked by how convincing I sound. Last night, all I wanted was to make love to him.

"Are you and Hercules able to be 'just friends,' though?"

The swimming pool comes to mind. Falling

asleep with my head on his chest does too. I want to be with him every second of the day. I can't wait until tonight. I've been counting the minutes.

Lake continues to watch me—and I can't look away from her. Her expression is the picture of curiosity.

She's about to say something else, but luckily, I'm saved by my chiming cellphone. It's Corina. She's transferred the full purchasing amount into an escrow account and has sent me documents to read over and sign. I could do it all on my cellphone, but I don't want to talk about my relationship with Hercules anymore. So I tell Lake I have to get home and handle the rest of the purchase. We hug, say we'll see each other soon, and I leave. If I stayed any longer, she would keep prying into my connection with Hercules, and I would eventually tell her the truth. At the moment, he's not just my friend. But I think the longer we deny our sexual desire for each other, the easier it will be to maintain a totally platonic relationship with each other.

"Never self-convince," I hear my dad say in my mind.

I groan as I stride up the Hudson Yards running path. "Shut up, Dad," I mutter and increase my pace.

# Girl Code

## PAISLEY GROVE

Covered in sweat, with my legs tight from running too fast, I enter my parents' penthouse. I stop in the massive foyer and press my palm over my rapidly beating heart. Suddenly I feel as though I'm existing outside my body, which makes me look down at my feet. Yes. I'm inside of myself and standing on the fourteen-carat gold honeycomb mosaic pattern etched into the marble floor. I look up at the crystal-encrusted chandelier above me. There's so much opulence surrounding me. The Grove family billions are all on display in this apartment in the sky. I always feel out of sorts when I walk inside this apartment. And I think I know why. It's my parents. Their residual energy is all over this place. Even though I live here alone, as long as I'm here, I reside under their watchful eye.

I start walking again, smiling from ear to ear. I'm on the verge of owning my own apartment, my first real piece of property that belongs totally to me. I make it to the office, fire up my iMac, and commence doing whatever needs to be done to complete the purchase so that I can get the hell out of here as fast as I can.

---

THE REST OF MY DAY IS A NAIL-BITER. FORTUNATELY, the deal between Davey Yee and me is crisp and clean. He paid cash for the apartment. And since I pay cash, too, things go fast. Now we're waiting for licensing, but as far as Davey is concerned, the place is mine. Lake had extra keys to his place, and he called her and told her to give them to me.

I call Treasure to ask what I should do next. She says she would come straight over and help me out herself, but she's on her way to Iceland because this morning she was offered a part in her fiancé's new *Game of Thrones*-style television show. She's playing a tribal princess.

I so very much want to voice my objection to that plan. She's already stretched thin with the restaurant, her clothing line, and her makeup brand, and now she's added acting to that. I'm worried about her. But I get it. Her dad has intercepted all payments from her grandfather's trust to her until she straightens up and flies right. Well, that's never going to happen. Since he cut her off, she hasn't been the same. Treasure misses the ease of having all that money. She won't take a loan from me because her pride gets in the way. She would rather run herself ragged than let me help her. She won't let Lynx, her older brother by one year, who's also cut off from his inheritance but doesn't need a dime of it because he owns a professional sports team, help her either. Basically, it's her pride that's sending her all the way to Iceland.

"But can you act?" I ask and then close my eyes to scold myself. I know that almost sounds like a criticism.

"Who gives a damn? Can Simon act? No," she replies curtly.

I remain silent until the best thing to say is, "Well, I'm going to miss you while you're gone." And then I tell her that I love her.

Regardless of not being here, she has told her

"team" to handle whatever I need. By four in the afternoon, I'm in place along with Reginald—an electrician—and his team, Ramsey from the alarm company, and Kelly, Treasure's interior designer, who is here to make suggestions. If I like her ideas, she'll make the changes. Apparently, Treasure doesn't like the fact that I've chosen to keep Davey's furnishings, but I wanted to move in quick. And I need furniture. But frankly, I like Davey's taste. Each piece of furniture has an artistic twist to it, and the bachelor-pad quality of the decor reminds me of Hercules's penthouse.

As the sky purples and then darkens, I realize that I've been so busy that I haven't thought much about Hercules. And since the new beds Kelly had ordered for me won't be in until Tuesday, and the cleaning services won't make the place spotless until Monday, I decide not to spend the night there. I head back to my parents' place.

I've stripped off my sticky clothes and showered and am sitting in bed with a big bowl of popcorn on my lap, getting ready to catch up on season one of the show Treasure has a new role in, when my phone rings.

"Yes," I say pumping my fist victoriously.

It's Hercules—finally. He's waiting for me at the rear of my building, at the loading dock.

———

AND NOW I'M WITH HERCULES. A PRIVACY SHIELD between the front and back seats separates us from James, the driver, who's taking us down city streets, weaving effortlessly through traffic. James is a skilled driver, as good as Greg, if not better.

I just finished telling Hercules I bought the apartment in Lake's building, and his frown hasn't yet eased. I thought he'd be happy for me because at least now we can see each other without the threat of my parents or Max ever catching us. But apparently, I was wrong.

"How much did you pay?" he asks.

I tell him.

"For that building? And it's really far, PG. Why didn't you tell me you were looking for a place to live?"

I frown, feeling as if I'm defending my purchase to Max and not my new friend Hercules Lord. "I did tell you." *Didn't I?*

"I don't remember."

I shake my head. "Maybe I didn't." I just feel

like I've shared more with him in the last few days than I have with any person other than Treasure.

He sighs briskly. "It's just that you'll be way down in Hudson Yards. I thought you wanted to keep this going."

I relax a bit now that I understand the real reason why he's so disappointed. "I do, but if I didn't buy the apartment today, then I would've lost it."

"I doubt that. For eight million? I wish you would've talked to me first."

I lean away from him, shocked by how angry he is about me buying my first home ever.

Hercules studies my grimace for a few beats and then rubs his hand over his mouth, effectively wiping away his frown. "Sorry. I'm overreacting, PG." My heart does a pirouette when he shows me my favorite lopsided smile. "We'll just have to get more creative about how and where we'll meet."

"I feel the loss too," I say before I know it. I'm usually too reserved to reveal something so personal and intimate. "I wish I'd thought about that beforehand."

Hercules's large, warm hand squeezes mine. "We'll figure it out."

Gazing into his eyes, I whisper, "You don't understand."

"What don't I understand?" His tone is tender, interested in whatever I have to say.

"It's been unbearable living in my parents' apartment. When I sent my eight million to the escrow account, I never felt so…" I close my eyes to search for the right words. "Adult. So free."

I open my eyes, and Hercules is staring at me as if my face is the only thing to look at in this world. I love it when he watches me that way. I have no doubt that he's into me. If only it weren't so difficult for us to be together.

Finally, Hercules's Adam's apple bobs as he swallows. "I understand. But…"

With my eyes pasted on his magnificent profile, I wait for him to finish. "But what?" I ask when he's paused for too long.

"Eight million is a lot of money. Wouldn't you have to clear the purchase with your parents?"

Sitting tall and feeling immense pride, I say, "No, I would not."

His eyebrows furrow. "Why not?"

"I have my own money. I'm paid royalties from Killer Firewall, and I also have my grandfather's trust, and I'm a fifteen percent owner of GIT."

"Wait. You created Killer Firewall?"

Suddenly, I realize that nobody knows I made the software. "Yeah."

His eyebrows raise in surprise. "Really?"

"Remember the Codearma competition in high school?"

He nods as a faraway look glistens his eyes. "Yes, you won. But your winning software wasn't Killer Firewall. It was, um… curriculum software for teachers."

I bite my lip, trying to keep my smile from growing even broader. "I can't believe you remember that."

His damp palm slides up and down the back of my hand. "I remember everything about you, PG."

*Oh, that was nice and flirtatious.* And his words and voice do the job—I'm trapped in his gaze. I want to grab his face and plant a long, hot kiss on his lips, but I can't.

Hercules's eyebrows pull into an intense frown. "By the way, you were going to tell me something last night but never finished."

I jerked my head back. "I was?"

"It was right before we landed. It seemed as though you wanted to say something about your grandfather."

I gasp as the memory returns so hard it feels like a sock to my brain. "Oh, yes."

His expression is open, patient. I'm contemplating whether I can trust him with what's been bothering me for many years. I mean, do I want to admit that I'm bothered by what I found? If I admit that what I found was wrong, that might mean my grandfather has done something bad.

I release a long sigh. "I found something," I start, trying on the words like a brand-new dress that might be too small. I want to sense how they feel leaving my mouth and whether I'm okay with saying more.

Hercules sits very still. His expression doesn't change as he continues to be patient, ready to hear it all.

"Letters," I say. I can hear my heart beating in my ears.

"Letters…?"

"To my grandmother from a man who called himself Garnet."

Hercules narrows an eye as he jerks his head back. "Garnet?"

"Yeah. They're love letters, and they're very old, written before my dad and uncle were born. I think my grandfather hid them away from my grandmother."

Hercules grunts as though he's fascinated by what I just revealed. "And did you read them?"

I swallow, and a heaviness sits in my chest. Then I sigh the weight out of me. "Every last one of them. They loved each other, this mystery man and my grandmother. It explains a lot, you know."

"What do you mean?" Hercules asks.

The air is still between us. I'm not sure what I'm feeling. *Betrayal? Relief?*

"My grandmother has rarely lived at home. She purports to be someone who was more married to her conservation cause than to my grandfather when he was alive, or even to her own children. But what if…?"

I close my eyes, trying to bear some of the distressing thoughts I've had for a long time. Hercules is still waiting silently. *Just say it, Paisley.*

"What if my grandfather kept my grandmother from marrying the man she truly loved?" I watch him with wide eyes, gnawing my bottom lip.

I'm hoping he'll say, "PG, it's probably nothing." But instead and very quickly, Hercules's face is near mine, and when his lips beckon, it feels as if the only right thing to do is to open up and let him into my mouth.

First, he sucks my lower lip. His warm tongue feels divine, and the sensation is so erotic. I've softened up, and I can't resist him as our kiss lingers for several seconds. Then he slips his tongue deeper into my mouth. Our kissing is intense, insatiable. Our moaning collides throughout the cab, and my hand finds its way to his package.

I whimper in his mouth, feeling how hard he is. I could unzip him, free his erection, and put it in my mouth. But…

He's squeezing my right breast when I break our lip contact and whisper, "Girl code."

Hercules's lips are still above mine when he says, "PG, you don't have to fall on your sword for Lauren."

"It's not about her. It's about me. And Lake and Treasure."

"I'm never going to marry her, PG." He sounds sure about that.

"You can't know that."

"I know it."

"Then break off the engagement right now."

We blink at each other. Instead of weakening,

our eye contact deepens. I'm asking him to do the impossible. But why? Hercules won't and can't break his commitment to Lauren, at least not tonight.

"We're here," James says.

"PG, give me time," Hercules whispers as the car stops.

"How much?" I ask.

"Not much."

Nodding, I swallow past my tight throat. "I'll try."

# Mr. Exciting

PAISLEY GROVE

Our first stop is a quaint neighborhood in Queens where the branches of trees curve over a quiet street. James gets out of the SUV in front of a gorgeous townhome, and then Hercules takes the wheel. I ride shotgun. We talk some more about what I read in those letters. Like, my grandmother and Garnet definitely had a lot of passionate sex. They cracked jokes together too. It was as if they had their own funny language. I told Hercules that my grandmother, as I've known her my whole life, has never been a humorous person.

"She told him everything about herself. Like I never knew my grandma lost her mother at an early age and that she was raised by her older sister. That kind of stuff. Very intimate."

Hercules reaches out for my hand, and I gave it to him. "What should I know about you, PG?"

I relax against the soft leather seat, feeling complete contentment. "There's not much to know." I turn to gaze at how the moonlight outlines his perfect profile. "I have no secrets other than you."

Hercules chuckles and squeezes my hand tighter. "Don't worry, PG. I plan on making an honest woman out of you."

I chuckle, thinking he's always made an honest woman out of me in my fantasies and dreams.

We arrive at a street festival in Long Island. Hercules explains that the festival sprang up unexpectedly, and the only people who know about it are those who can see it with their own eyes or those who received an invite from someone who knows about it.

My heart pumps at a feverish rate as Hercules and I stroll down the boardwalk of Rockaway Beach. If it weren't for the multicolored lit bunny ears we're wearing on top of rainbow wigs, people might recognize us—well, mainly him. Hercules always stands out like a sore thumb. He's tall, and the way his dark-gray pants caress his manly rear end and strong thighs distracts every woman who passes us. Not to mention his black button-down shirt made of expensive cotton material that shows off his biceps.

I can't imagine being Hercules Lord, a man whose genetics put him squarely at the top of the food chain as far as good looks go. However, Hercules doesn't seem to notice how others regard him. He's focused on me enjoying myself. And I am certainly enjoying myself.

It's as though we're smack-dab in the middle of Disneyland's festival of lights. We've played plenty of carnival games, like the one where the players lineup and shoot a clown in the mouth with water. Apparently, this causes a balloon to expand, and the first player to pop his or her balloon wins. Hercules wins of course. And since we've just arrived, we give the oversized panda bear to a little girl, who is over the moon about being given a stuffed animal that's almost bigger than she is.

Hercules promises to win me a prize bigger than the one he gave away, but I say, "Being with you is the biggest prize I can ever win."

We stare into each other's eyes yet again, waiting until the urge to kiss has passed. Then we stroll past all the sights and sounds of the lively festival as though we're very good friends who like each other a lot—like, a whole lot.

Every now and then, we stop to play another game. I win one, to the huckster's surprise. I've covered a large red circle with four metal rings. Apparently, the game is made for players to lose more than win. Upon my victory, Hercules and I find ourselves fighting the urge, yet again, to celebrate with a kiss. I hand my prize over to a cute little boy who's frustrated because he can't seem to beat the circle. I take a few minutes to show him exactly how I did it. Then Hercules and I watch as the kid wins his own prize.

After that, Hercules buys me my first funnel cake ever. I take a bite, and he grins as he watches me devour the rest. I've never eaten anything that fast in my life. I tell him how incredibly delicious the fried pastry was, so he buys me another one. But I take my time eating the second one as we stroll down the boardwalk, admiring the light-art master-pieces. We discuss which ones move us and why. Hercules so easily strikes up conversations with artists. Some of them have galleries in the city. He promises them that we'll visit them soon. Each time he says "we," I feel as if we're an item, and maybe tonight we are. Or maybe visiting art galleries is something friends do.

Then we dance. The night on my face—bliss in the air—I've never been happier. And wow, Hercules is an amazing dancer. His subtle hip swings are seductive and distracting. If he were giving me a striptease, all he'd have to do is take off his belt, and that would be it—job done. I'd be ready to grab him and beg him to make mad passionate love to me.

I put my mouth to his ear, and he raises his chin, waiting to hear what I have to say. "People are looking at us because of you."

Then he puts his mouth next to my ear, and that sends more tingles through my sex. "It's you they're looking at, PG. You're sexy as hell." He takes me by the hand. "But we should go before someone recognizes us and puts us in *Mag Rag*."

I chuckle. "You mean *Top Rag Mag*. Why can't you ever remember that?"

The look on his face is my answer. He doesn't remember the name of the magazine because he doesn't respect them.

And now my hand is in his. Everything inside me pumps harder as we walk back to his SUV, which is parked along the curb in front of beach homes. We stand in front of the passenger-side door. My head is tilted back and against the window. His face is over mine as our breaths crash into each other. We're silent. Our desire for each other is at an all-time high.

"I've been needing to kiss you," he whispers.

I swallow as chills simmer through me.

Hercules carefully wraps one arm around me. I can't step back or away from him. Instead, I let him guide me against his hard body. It's the dancing. He turned me on with his sexy moves. There's nothing I wouldn't do with him right now. He could bend me over, lay me against the seat, and pump into my wetness from behind. I'd blow him. I'd do whatever he wanted.

"But I know that if I push you to go too fast, you'll pull away," he says. "And I have a lot more nights like this in store for us."

I close my eyes, exhaling a shuddering breath out of my nose when I'm no longer in his arms. He reaches around me, the back of his hand his against my hip, his solid cock against me, as he opens the passenger-side door.

LATER ON, IN BED, I PICTURE HERCULES STANDING before me, at the door of his SUV, as Mr. Man mechanically brings me to climax. I scream in pleasure, but once my orgasm subsides, I throw my vibrator down on the empty mattress beside me. An orgasm did nothing to ease my yearning for the real thing. It's not the way he looks or the sex we've had that makes me want him so much. It's our conversations that I love, and the way I trust him makes me want to be with him forever. Maybe it isn't such a good idea to hang out with Hercules as I have been doing. I don't think we're capable of seeing each other platonically.

My cellphone beeps, and I flip onto my stomach to reach out and see who just sent me a message. I flip back onto my back after reading the screen.

*SLEEP WELL, PG.*

I PRESS MY DEVICE AGAINST MY HEART AND THEN text, *You too.*

Immediately, three animated dots show that he's typing a response. It's exciting to know that Hercules is somewhere in this dense metropolis, engaging with me. The dots go away and then come back again. I wait a few moments longer.

*THANK YOU*, HE SIMPLY REPLIES.

SIGHING AGAINST THE DARKNESS IN MY ROOM, I consider writing, *You're welcome*. But I know what I really want to say to him. But we can't meet up. We can't share a bed. We can't make love. That's why I put my phone on the nightstand, flip onto my side, and close my eyes.

I WAKE UP ON SUNDAY MORNING AND FEEL SO GOOD that I go for a run. As I stand in front of my parents' luxury apartment building, a weird feeling comes over me. Something's off. There's too much silence on a Sunday morning. My mom usually calls me at seven thirty on the dot, right before I suit up and go for a run. She likes checking in to ask whether I'm okay. "How's work? How's Max?" She never asks if I'm seeing anyone because she knows I'm not, and she never asks if I have any plans for the evening because, generally, she knows that I don't.

However, this morning, she hasn't called. That bothers me. I have to get the hell out of my parents' penthouse before they come knocking. Because the only time she doesn't call is when she shows up unannounced.

———

I DON'T EVEN SHOWER FIRST. I MUST LEAVE, AND fast. So I pack my things in two big rolling suitcases. I don't have much. I call a cab, but I think Hercules is right—now that *Top Rag Mag* is writing alerts about me, I should try to be safer about whose car I get into. Maybe I'll buy my own car. I haven't driven since after I graduated from college, when I worked as lead team member for product development for GIT in Palo Alto. Then I found the letters, my illusions about Grandfather were shattered, and I quit my job.

As I roll my suitcases into the private elevator and ride down to the lobby exit, I recall how I spent the next year with my grandmother on the wildlife preserve in Botswana. *Why didn't I tell her about the letters?* I've been trying to figure that out for a very long time. Regardless, within that year were some of the best days of my life—well, at least until now.

Being with Hercules feels like pure bliss. Swimming with him at his home in the Hamptons was thrilling. Dancing with him last night, playing games with him, and experiencing the sort of fun I should have experienced during my childhood feels revitalizing.

My cellphone rings just as the taxi stops in front of the valet station. I slide into the back seat, squinting at the screen. The call is from Max. I don't send him straight to voicemail because then he'll know that I've seen that he called. But I don't answer.

When I reach my new apartment building, I receive a second phone call. It's my dad. He must know that I bought an apartment. I don't answer his call either.

Before sliding out and heading into my new apartment, I break into a tiny smile. I feel truly free, even though I know that pretty soon all hell is about to break loose.

I STAND IN MY NEW LIVING ROOM, TAKING IT ALL IN. I bought everything in here.

The coffee table and the end tables resemble twisted silver licorice bites…

The sofa and chairs resemble large white marshmallows…

The large square black metallic coffee table…

I go closer and see that the top is an LCD screen with a small on-off square on edge. I tap it on. Blue lights that resemble lava swim through the tabletop. Smiling, I breathe in through my nose and blow out. All of this belongs to me.

The doorbell rings.

"I'm coming," I sing jubilantly and trot over to answer it.

The caller can only be one person, so I tug open the door, ready to explore more of the coffee table with Lake. But instead, I'm rendered wordless when I see who is there.

# Playing with Fire

## PAISLEY GROVE

Hercules has never looked so delectable. He's wearing athletic pants—the kind with a white stripe sewn on along each leg—and a brilliant-white V-neck T-shirt. The supple material clings to his powerful chest like a sensual kiss. And I just caught my first whiff of his cologne—an ambrosia of citrus, mint, and black licorice. *Delicious.*

"Hi," I say, feeling out of breath. I'm both surprised to see him and happy to be looking into his bright and smoldering eyes.

He's flashing me his winning smile. "Hey."

"How did you know I was here?"

"Mason."

I tilt my head back as if to say, "Ah." That's right—he's Mason's best friend.

Hercules rubs his palms together. "I would love to come in and take a look around. But we don't have time." He checks his watch.

Shimmers of excitement ripple across my face. "Why don't we have time?"

He winks. "I can't tell you. I have to show you."

———

SEVERAL HOURS LATER, HERCULES AND I ARE lounging on chaises, basking in the rays of a subdued afternoon sun, and sipping champagne. After we left my place together, which was a risky move on Hercules's part, he drove us to the building where we'd caught our first helicopter flight two nights earlier. We were flown to a super yacht anchored somewhere in the Hudson River. Hercules then showed me to a dressing room, where I had my pick of a collection of never-worn bathing suits.

I chose a red one-piece instead of a bikini. I figured that would send a message that I wasn't trying to arouse him, even though if I was being completely honest with myself, I would have to admit I wanted to arouse him.

When I met Hercules on the top deck by the swimming pool, he froze. The way he looked at me made me feel like the most beautiful girl in the world. We stood locked in an intense stare before Hercules cleared his throat and said he was going to check on lunch.

As we ate, we talked about that New Year's Eve years ago. But though the conversation was about us, Eden and Nero were at the top of the discussion. Hercules recounted the same story that Eden had told me—the two of them went swimming in his uncle's heated pond, and then they talked until morning.

He asked if I minded passing Eden's number to him so his cousin could have it. Apparently, he'd used the possibility of getting the number to make Nero go easy on me last Thursday. Finding that funny, I laughed and then messaged him Eden's number.

After finishing our filet mignon and lobster, we swam. Now we're drying off, catching up on the last seven years of our lives. I tell him more about my days spent on the wildlife preserve with my grandmother. I share stories about my favorite animals and how I made friends with a family of wild dogs and hyenas. Hercules is totally engrossed in whatever I have to say. He laughs on cue, especially when I tell him how a baby elephant fell in love with me, and his mother had to continually save me from his affection.

"Animals are just as smart as we are," I say. "What about you? How did your life progress after I gave you my virginity?"

Hercules laughs, and his eyes gleam. I think he likes that he was my first just as much as I like it. Then he tells me that after finishing his undergrad studies, he took two more years to complete an MBA. After that, he needed a break, so he traveled for a year, starting in Tokyo then traveling across Asia and parts of North Africa.

"I'd already traveled through Europe ad nauseam. My mother considered it a badge of honor to send us to Europe every summer."

He visited holy sites, made friends, and sat down for dinner with families he'd just met. He hiked a lot, swam in the ocean, and attended festivals.

"What about girls? Did you fall in love?" My heart sinks a bit. I don't even know the answer, and I'm already jealous.

An easy smile spreads across his supple lips as his eyes dance around my face. "No, PG." Then his eyebrows shoot up. "Actually, there weren't a lot of single girls my age in those countries. At least, I had no access to them. But I wasn't looking to get my cock wet. I wanted to learn more about people other than those I already knew."

We're smiling at each other for no reason other than that perhaps we're falling in love. And I don't want to think about the danger in that—not right now. Then he invites me into the hot tub, which has been brewing for us, and I say yes.

Once we're surrounded by the bubbling water, Hercules says, "Thank you for spending this day with me, PG."

"Thank you for planning it and inviting me."

He shakes his head gently. "You don't ever have to thank me for anything I do for you, PG. It's my pleasure."

We're doing it again—staring at each other, saying "I love you" with our eyes. I break eye contact first to gaze at the crackling bubbles the jets are kicking up. Then I remember something I meant to ask him about.

I look up. He's still gazing at me. "Did you know that Mason passed out on Friday evening?"

His expression transforms into one of surprise. "No."

I feel as though I might have revealed something to him that Lake or her fiancé didn't want him to know. "Oh," I say, frowning. "I'm not sure if I should've told you."

"You definitely should've told me. Do you know why he passed out?"

I press my lips together, remembering how blasé Lake and Mason were being about the whole ordeal. "They think it's stress."

Hercules's eyes brows crash into an intense frown. "He has been working hard. But—did he get checked out by a doctor?"

I'm so glad Hercules asked me that. That was exactly what I asked Lake. I wonder why Mason wouldn't just go to the doctor. I would have if I'd passed out. Many people are stressed out, and they don't pass out while walking to the bathroom.

"No," I finally say. "He doesn't think he has to go to the doctor."

"The hell he doesn't. I'll call him tonight." Hercules looks concerned.

I love that he cares about someone so much. I wish he weren't the person I've always known him to be—the man who's a gift from God.

"Is he working too hard, though?" I ask.

Hercules gazes off thoughtfully. "He is. We both are. If I weren't with you, I'd be sleeping right now."

"Oh." I drop my head. I have thoughts, but I'm not sure if I should speak them. "Maybe I can help." I quickly look up.

Curiosity is in his eyes.

"Maybe I can help you come up with a product that will expand in the marketplace. My grandfather used to say that a company doesn't need many products—it only needs one good one."

Hercules's face twists and twitches, and he sniffs like a mad bull. I'm worried. I hope I haven't insulted him.

"That's not why I'm with you, PG," he hisses.

I take a minute to figure out why he said that. "You're not actually with me, though. You're with Lauren. However, you and I are becoming better friends. And friends help friends, don't they?"

Hercules's expression is blank, but it's more than just unreadable. It's like he's made his face unreadable on purpose. Maybe I hurt him with my words. I didn't mean to. I only meant to be practical, walk down the only road that's available to us, and not linger on the one that isn't. That's my dad's philosophy, not my grandfather's.

"No, thank you. I'll figure it out myself."

The silence between us feels different. It's not laced with desire, lust, and want. I feel as though at any moment, he's going to check his watch and say we should go. But in an instant, his face shows me a brand-new expression.

"I am attracted to you, PG," he says. "There's no doubt about it. I also want to be very honest with you."

I swallow hard and nod. With one swift movement, Hercules moves right in front of me. He clutches the edge of the hot tub, arms extended past my shoulders.

"I like being your friend. I believe friendship is a solid foundation for any great love affair. But I'm not looking to sit in your friend zone forever. Got it?"

His lips are so close. And his erection has broken out of his swimming trunks. We both bend our necks to see it poking me in my lower abs.

"Oh, I'm getting it," I say, noting the sheer size and width of his cock.

We laugh, staring intently into each other's eyes. *It would be so easy, wouldn't it?* All I'd have to do is pull the crotch of my swimsuit to one side and let him slide in. Then I'd be full of Hercules Lord. I'd embrace him tightly as his pleasure-bringing cock pumped in and out of me.

I force myself to say, "But really, Hercules, can you absolutely say that you will defy your family if need be and not marry Lauren?"

His Adam's apple bobs as he whispers thickly, "It won't come to that, PG."

His cock has dropped lower, and now it's pressing against my hood. Hercules is beyond hard. I want him to do it so much, but he didn't actually say he would defy his family.

"Why won't it come to that?" I ask.

"Because I'm smart."

I close my eyes and shake my head. "That makes no sense."

"I'll find a way."

"A way not to marry your cousin so that your family can be paid more money from the Lord Trust?"

"Yes."

I feel like nudging him in the chest and pushing him away from me. "Do you have a solution?"

Tension comes to his mouth. The way he's

looking into my eyes changes. I think I've hit a nerve.

Finally, he pushes himself away from me and sits where he'd been before trying to tempt me into sex. "Not yet."

I close my eyes and inhale deeply through my nose. I'm not sure what just happened. Scratching the back of my head, I'm certain it's time for logical deduction.

"Okay, Hercules, do you really want to be my friend, or is all of this about you trying to seduce me?" I keep my expression serious, showing him that I'm not playing games here.

He's silent, watching my face. "Both," he finally says, appearing just as serious as I am.

I sigh with relief. "Well, sex is not an option as long as you're engaged."

"That's clear."

"So, do you want to stop hanging out?"

He barely shakes his head and whispers, "No." Then he clears his throat. "I don't ever want to stop hanging out with you."

# The Ticking Clock

## PAISLEY GROVE

O n Monday morning, I make it to my office at eight o'clock. Now I'm resting my head on my desk, trying to catch at least ten minutes of extra shuteye before my first meeting of the day. After our talk about being friends, Hercules asked why I hadn't ever told my grandmother about the letters I found.

"I don't know." But just as soon as I'd given him the glib answer the truth sat on the tip of my tongue. "Because I don't want to ruin the illusion," I confessed.

"What illusion?" Hercules asked.

My shoulder rose high as I inhaled deeply. Then I slowly released the air from my lungs. "Because I want to believe that at some level, my grandparents truly loved each other, and my dad and Leo were born out of that real love," I said tightly, fighting severe sadness. "But I'm thinking that Leslie and Charles were married out of obligation."

"Obligation to what?"

I shook my head as I tried yet again to figure out what my grandfather knew that made my grandmother choose him instead of the other man. "I don't know. But I believe the choice she made had something to do with protecting this Garnet man. And I don't think his real name is Garnet because I tried to find him but I couldn't. I could find anyone in the world if I wanted to."

Lust and appreciation shaped his tapered eyes. "That I know for sure," he said in a husky voice that melted my panties.

I looked away from him to blush, and when I set my dazzled eyes back on Hercules, he told me all about how he used to sit in meetings at work and think, "Paisley Grove would know how to solve this or that problem." He even wrestled the desire to reach out to me a few times, he had said.

"The only reason I didn't is that I thought you'd have a boyfriend or fiancé or someone. I was never ready to learn that you were with another man."

I admitted the same was true for me. I never

wanted to know anything about his personal life. It would've distressed me for years to come to have known that Hercules was engaged to Lauren.

I told him that. I even confessed that it was a struggle to see him platonically and that it might be best if we kept our distance until he came up with a solution to officially cut ties with his distant cousin.

"But PG," he said. "The more we see each other platonically, the sooner we might get past whatever this is that makes us want to—you know—make love."

"That will never work," I whisper, remembering how as soon as I got home, I grabbed Mr. Man and fantasized about Hercules stroking, licking, touching me, and kissing me until the point of orgasm.

"What won't work?" Max's voice booms through my office.

I don't lift my head right away. Gosh, he sounds so miserable. *Will my brother ever be happy?*

My eyelids are heavy when I finally look at him. "Good morning to you too."

Max crosses his arms and widens his stance. "Why didn't you answer my calls?"

I massage my temples, realizing that my head didn't ache until he showed up. "Because I didn't want to be bothered."

Suddenly, Max bolts forward and flops down in a chair across from me. "I'm not in the mood, Paisley."

I glare at him defiantly. "Well, neither am I." And that's the truth.

"Why the hell didn't you do what you were advised to do at the hearing? You put us at a disadvantage."

"I didn't perceive there was any disadvantage to answering the arbiter's questions."

He glares at me. He's angry. Max is not one to shout or lose control. Scathing eye contact always does the slicing and dicing for him. "Listen, Pais, it's time you go back to head of product development."

I feel like a deer trapped by headlights. "But…"

"Hey…" a gloriously soft voice sings.

Max whips himself around to see Lake standing in my doorway. She's my 9:15 a.m. And I've never been so happy to see her. It looks like all the blood has drained from my brother's face as he seems to thoughtlessly rise to his feet.

"I'm sorry, am I interrupting?" Lake asks, looking like a vision in a white halter dress with red leather closed-toe sandals.

"Not at all." I observe Max closely. He's watching her with ruffled eyebrows as though he can't figure out whether he's attracted to the woman who just crashed his lambasting of his heady younger sister, or irritated about her intrusion.

"We'll talk later," he says to me, but he can't take his eyes off my friend.

Lake shoots me a look as if to ask what the hell is wrong with your brother and then musters a friendly smile for him. "Good morning, Max."

His gaze laps her face. I'm wondering if he's going to say anything at all until he grumbles, "Good morning."

"Oh," she says and snaps her fingers as if she's just remembered something. "Paisley told me you liked *Pillows Through the City*, and you have it hanging in your office." She leans toward him as if she's inviting him on a secret. "I just want to say thanks. I appreciate that you like my work."

*He's not going to smile*, I think. And he doesn't. Max nods briskly and then escapes fast. When he's out of sight, Lake and I look at each other with wide, stunned eyes.

"Your brother is odd." She walks over and sits in the chair Max abandoned.

"True. But he also likes you," I say, stating the obvious. "Maybe I should tell him that you're getting married."

Lake splays her fingers over her chest. "He likes me? No way. I never attract guys like your brother, never. They're scared of me."

Chuckling, I say, "Oh, yes, he's into the artistic types." I slouch as I yawn. "Max has never had many girlfriends. He's only introduced me to one, and she was a serious artist."

Lake perks up. "She lives in the city?"

"Yep."

She tosses her head into a tilt. "Oh, really? What's her name?"

"Kiera Langford."

She gasps into her palm. "I know Kiera." She shrugs. "Well, *knew* her."

My heart feels as if it's free-falling. "Did something bad happen to her?"

"No," she repeats, shaking her head adamantly. "Nothing bad."

I'm seeing all the signs of exhaustion on Lake's face as she tells me that Kiera left the New York art scene four years ago. She now lives in Long Island and has three kids. She's no longer a platinum blonde with dreadlocks either.

We fall silent. I'm not sure what Lake is thinking, but I'm trying to picture Kiera without her long blonde dreads and oversized painted, stained coveralls. The vision won't materialize in my mind. Seeing her that way is sort of beyond comprehension.

"She wanted Max to settle down with her," I say. "But he wasn't ready to give her that. That's why she broke up with him."

"I never would have guessed your brother was commitment-phobic."

I twist my mouth thoughtfully. "I wouldn't say he's commitment-phobic. He's just way too ambitious for his own good."

She watches me curiously and with intense focus. "Is that so?"

"Yep."

"Ambitious about what?"

I wish I could say TRANSPOT, but I can't, since Lake is engaged to the competition. "Work," I say instead. Then I quickly scoot to the edge of my seat. I don't want to talk about Max anymore. Plus, his old girlfriend, who I liked very much, is still on my mind. "But Kiera, is she happy?" I ask, wanting desperately to hear that she is.

Lake sits up straight and blinks a few times. I think I hit her too hard with my effort to change the subject. "By the looks of it, yes," she says. "But one can never know unless you know, you know?"

I snort, smiling. "I know." Then I remember that yesterday morning when she called to tell me that she found Davey's keys, she had something to tell me. "By the way, what did you want to talk to me about?"

Gradually, a veil of sadness transforms her happy expression.

"What is it?" I'm feeling worried.

"Mason and I have decided to postpone the wedding."

I jerk my posture up a tad bit straighter. "Why?"

She sits very still and closes her eyes. Soon, tears roll down the side of her face.

"Oh no." I reach for the box of tissues at the corner of my desk and place it in front of her.

Lake snatches a tissue our of the box and blows her nose. "He's been having these fainting spells. We thinks it's stress." She takes another tissue and dabs her eyes with it. "He's also mad at me for taking this assignment."

The corners of my mouth turn down as I think about all that's changed in my life since Lake and I became acquainted. "I'm glad you took the job."

Lake manages to smile again. "So am I. But I can't ignore Mason's health these days. Sometimes I look at him, and I swear he's anemic. I've never seen him this way. I'm worried, Paisley. And he refuses to go to the doctor." She forces a breath out of her nose as she shakes her head. "He can be so stubborn. It's the one thing about him that irks me. But we agreed to postpone the wedding until things get better."

I nod supportively. "That makes sense."

The way Lake is watching me with wide open eyes and pressed lips is making me nervous. "What is it?"

"There's something else."

---

*WHO ARE THOSE PEOPLE AT* Top Rag Mag*? Don't they have anything better to do than follow Hercules and me around?*

Their attempt to derive amusement from my life seems borderline cruel. Some spy has captured us in the hot tub yesterday. The video makes the one moment when Hercules and I almost succumbed to our lusts appear more salacious than what actually happened between us. And then there's the blurb written underneath the video…

> *Look what happens when the heir and heiress think nobody's watching. Oh, we here at Top Rag Mag have eyes everywhere, even in the murky green water of the Hudson River.*
>
> *And for the record, we graciously withdraw Friday's retraction. This little rendezvous proves that our street team had not gotten their hands on any doctored video. These two are doing it and doing it, and, well… you know the rest.*
>
> *But I don't see what the big deal is, do you? This couple is hot, hot, hot.*
>
> *Oh…*
>
> *That's right.*
>
> *He's engaged.*
>
> *#Messy*

I close my eyes as embarrassment flushes through me.

"You were with him yesterday," Lake says. I detect a hint of criticism.

"I was. But we're just friends."

"Oh, Paisley," she says, shaking her head. "It's kind of like two sugar addicts staring down a birthday cake?"

My lips are stuck closed as I visualize a cake.

"Just because you're practicing restraint doesn't

mean you won't end up burying your faces in the dessert," Lake concludes.

I squish my face, picturing Hercules and me standing on each side of his king-sized bed. The bed is the cake. We want to get naked. We fall onto the mattress and the rest is history.

"Right," I say faintly, feeling flushed.

Lake observes me. I'm guessing that my skin is patchy and my eyes wired from desire.

"Be careful, Paisley. I don't want you to get hurt."

I tell her I'll be careful, and then we start our meeting, finalizing her renderings for the upcoming benefit.

# Caught

HERCULES LORD

I've been summoned to my mother's house in Greenwich, Connecticut. I pushed to learn the topic of discussion, but she said, "Not over the phone." The Lord family estate resides in the backcountry of Greenwich, Connecticut. I pushed my meetings back to after lunch, and the only way to make it back in time for them without overextending myself is to helicopter out to Greenwich.

I should be landing soon, but for most of the ride, I've been wondering if somehow my family caught wind of the fact that I continued seeing Paisley. I hope not. I'm not ready to back away from her.

The thought of leaving her alone reminds me

that my body aches. I circle my shoulders to loosen them. I might have done too much swimming in the past three days. I'm a runner. I don't exercise the muscle group I use for swimming that much.

Also, I swam more than Paisley did, overexerting myself to rid myself of the urge to pump my cock into her hot wetness. She gets so damn wet for me. I kept fighting the urge to put my lips and tongue on her shoulder and suck. Her skin is soft. Her kiss is too. Her mouth tastes sweet.

I rub up and down my cock. Thoughts of Paisley Grove never fail to make me hard. I've wondered if I would think about Paisley as much as I do if she would just let me pound her out of my system.

*Could I pound her out of my system? I don't think that I can.*

On Thursday night, I felt a thrill, learning that she let me come inside her all those years ago. I wouldn't have minded if I'd gotten her pregnant. Then there would have been nothing anyone could say about us being together. She'd be mine. And what if we'd married and had more children? I think we would be happy. I know we would be happy.

I sink deeper into my seat as I stare, unfocused, at the dense green layering the landscape below. In my mind's eye, I see Xander Grove clearly—his light hair, square chin, and glasses that make him look smarter than the rest of us. I ask him for his daughter's hand in marriage. I plead my case, saying she's been back in my life for less than a week, but I've loved her since high school. I can't picture what Xander Grove says to me, but he doesn't say no, at least not in my fantasy.

"What will Paisley and I do tonight?" I whisper.

I can't wait to see her pretty face again.

---

THE HELICOPTER TOUCHES DOWN ON LANDING PAD number two. I eye the silver helicopter sitting idle on landing pad number one. It belongs to Achilles.

The door opens, and the steps lower automatically. The exit light flashes green. Ducking my head, I disembark, muttering a string of curse words.

My brother wouldn't take time out of his busy Monday morning for breakfast at our mother's if the topic of discussion wasn't about money. These days, if I'm part of the conversation and it doesn't have anything to do with LTI, then it'll have something to do with me marrying Lauren. Managing her would be easy if she didn't want to marry me.

Flanked by tall trees that stand at attention, I scowl at the cobblestone walkway that leads to the rear-door entrance. I'm worried because my steps sound too indecisive. I'll admit that I'm nervous. I've been negligent recently. The truth of the matter is that I almost accepted marrying Lauren. She's attractive. She's nice enough, although I'm not attracted to her. Lauren doesn't open up about herself much—actually, not at all. But I can understand a person who keeps her cards to herself. However, she has one trait that irks me to no end. Whenever we're out together at parties or even dinner, she likes to comment on people's flaws. She'll point out a dress and say that it's cheap. She'll criticize a woman for wearing what she calls bad makeup or say that another woman's heels are too high, even though hers are pretty high too.

She even made a string of negative comments about Paisley during the party on Thursday night. I can only recall a few of the comments she made about her because I was too focused on Paisley dancing with Lake. They were sexy moving together. I would never cross the line by picturing my best friend's fiancée naked, but Lake's moves were as almost as sensual as Paisley's. The difference, the one that made Paisley the ultimate winner, was that Lake tried harder to be appealing, but Paisley's sex appeal was natural.

*Damn… making love to her is addictive.*

But Lauren referred to Paisley as an eye whore and then explained that Paisley wanted every man in the room to pay attention to her. I was too confused by her judgment to say something in Paisley's defense. That wasn't PG at all. At least, that wasn't how I remembered her. I tried to notice everything about PG as she danced—the way she gyrated her sexy hips, raised her hands above her head, and twisted her body down toward the floor. Watching her as if in a trance got me hard. Then I watched other men admiring her. She was getting a lot of attention. But just like the PG I remembered, she didn't notice. When she started dancing with Clive Alden, I nearly lost my composure. He kept putting his hands on her, touching her waist and her arms, and leaning into her. My jealousy soared through the roof. Then she shuffled off the dance floor.

"Be right back," I said to Lauren.

Of course, I never went back. The next morning, Lauren's phone call woke me up. I lied to her. I told her I was called away on business.

"What business?" she snapped.

"Personal business."

"Did your business have to do with that girl in the red dress?"

"No. She wouldn't be business. She'd be pleasure." That was the truth.

I could feel Lauren's gasp through the phone.

"You can be such an asshole, Hercules. You better get it together because like it or not, we're getting married." Then she briskly said goodbye and ended our call.

That's the thing that baffles me the most. Lauren should be pissed that she has to marry a man she only met two months ago. I remember the night our families sailed on Achilles's yacht in the Hudson Bay. She cornered me while I was taking a piss. My cock was out, and she dropped to her knees and tried to put me in her mouth.

It's often said that no guy turns down a blow job. But I did. My father's words echoed in my head: "Sex with a woman is never free."

I'm glad I had the willpower to stop her. But the clincher was, later that night, I caught her topping off Orion in the hot tub. Head underwater, she was holding her breath while taking him into her mouth.

Arms spread across the rim of the hot tub and head tilted back, Orion sighed and said, "Damn, you're an expert, baby."

Of course, he would do a woman who was supposed to belong to me. The only reason he hasn't made a move on PG is that she's Treasure's cousin. She's the only woman he's ever given a damn about.

However, neither Orion nor Lauren knows I caught her blowing him. I figured it would take her a while to get him off, being that a person can only hold her breath underwater for so long. I hurried back to my cabin, retrieved my cellphone, and waited for him to be done humiliating her by making her struggle to blow him with her head underwater. Orion likes doing shit like that, making women sink to depths so low just to have him. I think Treasure Grove flipped his script on him, though.

When he finally stood so Lauren could finish him off, I captured them on video. According to the Lord Trust rules, sucking my brother's cock makes her ineligible to be my wife. What I captured will come in handy one day and maybe sooner than I think. It all depends on how things go with Achilles this morning.

The inside of the mansion I grew up in is impressive and too large for a family our size, and now that my mom lives here alone, it's especially too big for one person. My footsteps echo through the wide gallery hallway as I walk on the travertine marble floor on my way to the dining room. The closer I get, the easier it is to smell breakfast mingling with fresh coffee. Oddly, the scent puts me at ease. It reminds me that I'm home. My mom is never my enemy. Sure, she's motivated by money, but still, if any of my family members can be swayed to take a new path toward the same goal, it's her.

I love my mother. And I believe I'm Marigold Lord's favorite son. That's why, when I enter the dining room, she leaps to her feet, holding Fifi, her fluffy white bichon frise, who's barking and wagging her tail. I'm Fifi's favorite son too.

"Hercules, you made it, my love," my mother sings.

I ignore the way Achilles, who's seated across from the place setting that's waiting for me, scowls at his cellphone as I close the distance between our mother and me.

"Good morning, Mother." I kiss her on the cheek. Fifi jumps into my arms and licks my face.

"All right, enough," Achilles says sourly. "Let's get this over with. I have meetings, and so do you."

I snort a laugh without humor. This guy, this brother of mine, can't exist without being controlling. I fight the urge to resist him. But he's right. I do have meetings. Plus, I'm curious about why I'm here.

I hand Fifi back to my mother, where she's happiest. The dog has lost all her excitement too. Even Fifi knows to fall in line when Achilles starts barking orders.

"Good morning to you too," I say snidely as I take my seat.

Achilles grimaces at his phone as his finger works the screen. A server I've never seen before pours me coffee. My mother goes through servers like they're potato chips.

"Thanks," I say. "And your name...?"

"My name is Bailey," the kid replies. He looks to be in his early twenties.

My mom has a way of chastising her house staff with her eyes, which is what she does with Bailey after he tells me his name.

"Thanks, Bailey. What are you doing in these parts?" I ask him.

His eyes grow wide. He doesn't know that if my mom fires him, I might hire him. Working for her isn't a great gig. She's high-maintenance and can be impolite. And to compensate for being lonely out here in the middle of nowhere, she will pick at the staff just to interact with people.

"Bailey, leave us," Achilles says.

Bailey seems happy to get the hell out of here.

"What's this?" Achilles asks.

I focus on my brother again. He's holding up his cellphone. I squint at a video of me in the hot tub with Paisley yesterday evening. It was the moment when I could hardly stand the distance between us, so I closed it. Damn, I wanted her so bad. I'm starting to wish I'd nibbled her neck to see what she would've done.

"Where did you get that?" I ask, even though I recognize the signage from *Rag Mag*.

Achilles sneers. "You see, Hercules, you're asking the wrong fucking question."

The sarcasm in his voice makes me snort. I scoot to the edge of my chair, look him dead in the eyes, and ask, "Okay, then, tell me—what's the right question to ask?"

Achilles's eyebrows snap upward. I stop myself from smirking in victory. He expected me to back down and cower to him so we could commence the process of me being his whipping boy. But that's not going to happen. Not this time. And actually, I'm surprised by how committed I am to defying him.

Achilles snarls at me. "You believe you have a choice in this matter, don't you?"

"I didn't know you were seeing the Grove daughter—the smart one," my mother says out of the blue.

I flinch at my mother referring to Paisley as the smart one. It sounds as though she likes hearing that I'm involved with Paisley. And now that I think about it, I'm not surprised. I might not have known Paisley created Killer Firewall, but I know goddamn well she knows.

My mother rubs her fingers through Fifi's luxurious coat, and her brows furrow thoughtfully. "Xander Grove and Heartly Grove's daughter. She's the one who's responsible for Killer Firewall."

I snort because I knew it.

"I understand that you and Paisley Grove have gotten very close," my mom says, still stroking Fifi as though she hasn't an ounce of anxiety coursing through her, given the subject at hand. That's how I know she's plotting. "But that stops now. Unless…"

"There's no unless, Mother," Achilles snaps.

"Unless," my mother pushes forward defiantly, "there's an advantage to you keeping her company for the time being."

"No!" Achilles and I roar at the same time. We glare at each other. Rarely are we on the same page.

"Are you seriously asking me to keep seeing her, hoping I'd get something out of her?"

"Yes," my mother says as if there's no shame in her game.

Achilles aims his finger at me. "I want you to stay away from Paisley Grove."

My right eye narrows to a slit as I consider how badly I want to rip his head off. But he's the one who's making the right call if the goal is to keep our families separate. Achilles understands the depths of how much I care about Paisley. He's seen her red dress splayed on the floor in my den. I'm pretty sure Lauren has called him and complained about how I left her at the party to be with Paisley. Spending more time with Paisley will only make us closer. It will destroy any plans of me eventually marrying Lauren, and Achilles is smart enough to get that.

"And I'm going to show you why." Achilles is composed as he reaches over to take a manila folder off the cushion of the chair beside him. "I will remove you as the head of LTI for good if you don't straighten up and stop jeopardizing our future."

The folder drops right in front of my empty plate. He made a perfect toss. I frown at the folder, circle my shoulders back, and then open it. There are legal documents inside. I'll have to read them closely to get the gist of Achilles's threat. My brother doesn't make empty threats, so I'm certain the documents back up his claim.

"I'm starving. Let's eat." My mom uses her forefinger and thumb to delicately lift and ring a silver bell.

The servers in white jackets roll breakfast in on silver carts. The food smells and looks good. Too bad I lost my appetite.

# Turning Points

## PAISLEY GROVE

## TUESDAY

When my eyes blink open, daylight surrounds me. I quickly sit up and then swipe my cellphone off the coffee table. There's no call from Hercules, and it's 10:37 a.m. I overslept. But since my beds are being delivered today, I'm scheduled for three remote teleconference meetings. My first is scheduled to start at eleven o'clock.

It's 9:37 a.m. and I have twenty-three minutes to prepare for my first conference call of the day which is with Accounting. As I hook my laptop up to an external monitor in my home office, I received a message from Ru.

I read: *Your meetings have been canceled. And I've been reassigned to support a new executive effective immediately. Thank you for everything you've done for me. Working with you has been like Blue Cherry pie. I heard you're going back to product development. Congratulations.*

My mouth falls open. "What the hell?" No I'm not. Max is insistent on starting a war with me. I'm not ready to go back to product development and he can't make me do it. *And why is Ru speaking to me in code?*

Blue Cherry is a bar she and I often visit after a long day at the office. It's our favorite place to go to wind down and reset. I'm certain she's asking me to meet her there, perhaps today by six o'clock. That's at least an hour after she leaves the office.

My phone beeps again, and I raise it to read the message. Max wants me to report to the eighth floor today at two o'clock to meet and brief the TRANSPOT team.

*Have something prepared*, he tells me.

I laugh harshly. Middle finger up, I flip off my phone. I hope Max doesn't hold his breath waiting for me to show up to that meeting.

## HERCULES LORD

I haven't slept a bit since Sunday, except for when I closed my eyes while sitting at my desk. At the time, I drifted off and then jerked my head up before I tipped forward, back, or to either side. For the most part, the atmosphere has been transitioning through its regular fluctuations from day to night, but I have been up, putting it all together, finding answers.

I check the time and date at the corner of my computer—Tuesday, 1:43 p.m. It feels as though I just ended Sunday breakfast with my mother and Achilles, who left after he made sure I had the bad news he delivered in my hands.

I haphazardly listened to my mother prattle on about design changes she was making to the interior and exterior of the estate as though she hadn't partnered with Achilles in upending my peace of mind. When I was done eating, instead of getting the hell out of there, I went to the more private study located at the rear of the house, a room that was rarely used, and read over the documents Achilles tossed at me. As of this coming Friday, the marriage between Lauren Ivy Mueller and Hercules Ivan Lord will be legal. All parties have agreed and signed. Achilles forged my signature. I bet he's daring me to contest the signature. I won't, simply because I'm taking a different route to get what I want. And I think I can make it work. It would have been an uphill battle if I hadn't seen what I saw in the rear wing's study.

*Damn, how lucky can one man get in fewer than seven days?* After that, I thought, *It's time to fight Achilles's kind of fire with molten lava.*

I'd never before gone through the Lord Trust with a fine-toothed comb. I never felt motivated enough to do it. But now I am. Not only have I read the five hundred pages of trust rules from cover to cover, but I've done it twice. And my efforts have paid off.

That's why my headache and body stiffness feel so damn good. I have found something that will liberate our clan of Lords from jumping through my great-grandfather's holier-than-thou hoops. My plan involves the Groves. I took a picture of the painting hanging on the wall in the study.

I rub my temples. My head hurts so badly—my brain feels like it wants to burst. But I've done a good job. That's what my grandfather would tell me if he knew all the steps I'd taken to get to this point.

Achilles will be butthurt at first, but eventually, he'll appreciate the work I put in. Orion, well... maybe he'll be ready to do some of the heavy lifting for once. We'll see.

# *On Paper*

### ❦

PAISLEY GROVE

The beds have been dropped off and set up. Keeping busy with that has made me forget the catastrophe that is my career. It's three in the afternoon. In three hours, I'm to meet Ru at the Blue Cherry. Standing in the middle of my living room after everyone is gone, I breathe in deeply, filling my chest with air and holding it for one, two seconds, and then slowly release it.

That settles me. I'll have to plan my next steps.

*But why hasn't Hercules called?*

"Maybe I should call him," I whisper and take steps toward my phone, which sits on top of the coffee table. But then I stop to search my body for physiological responses.

Maybe not. Maybe space between us is what we need right now.

Someone knocks on my door. Thinking it's Lake, I race over to open it. My jaw drops. "Oh."

Max holds up a paper bag with something that smells warm, delicious, and familiar. "I come in peace," he says, taking a stab at a sincere smile.

---

MAX BROUGHT MY FAVORITE—A BARBECUE CHICKEN salad sandwich from Delta's Grill. I make us cappuccinos with the fancy barista-style cappuccino and coffee maker installed in the kitchen. So far, Max has been on his best behavior. He's only asked me questions about Lake. I hate to thwart his hopes, but I let him know that she's getting married soon to Mason, who of course my brother knows.

Max is always hard to read when it comes to matters of the heart. It's hard to even suss out whether he likes or hates someone. Usually, I know how he feels by what he does. As they say, actions speak louder than words—or in his case, facial expressions.

"But they're putting it off because Mason hasn't

been feeling well lately." I hand him a white porcelain cup topped with the creamiest foam.

Max's bottom lip pouts thoughtfully as he rubs it.

"Do you like her?" I sit on the white marshmallow-like sofa. Despite its pretty form, it's not very comfortable.

"Not if she's getting married. And maybe you should follow my lead." He raises a thick dark and naturally manicured eyebrow.

*Here we go.* Although I'm not going to lie to myself—I love sitting with Max while I eat my favorite sandwich and drink the cappuccino I made for us. It's been too long since we've done this. In the past, we sat down together a lot and shared a meal. Max and I have always found something to talk about. Not many people get to see or engage with this side of him—the likable side.

"You don't have to warn me about, Hercules. We're just friends."

Chin lowered, he studies me with critical eyes as he takes a sip of his cappuccino. No words are needed. That's his way of saying, "You're not fooling me or yourself."

"So, why are you here, Max?" I say, briskly readjusting in my seat.

"You missed the meeting. Why?"

I keep my expression even. "I never agreed to work with the TRANSPOT team. And with all due respect, I'm not letting you bully me into it."

"No one's bullying you, Paisley."

I grunt facetiously. "You want me to count the ways?"

Max sets the cappuccino on the coffee table. "You used to like trying to figure out TRANSPOT. What happened?"

I want to spill my guts about the letters that point at Grandfather deceiving Grandmother into marrying him—how she was in love with this Garnet person. But maybe Max already knows.

"Have you ever heard of someone named Garnet?" I ask.

His expression doesn't budge. "Garnet? No."

Even though his poker face might be hiding something, I believe him.

"Do you think Grandmother and Grandfather were in love?"

"No," he says without pause.

I'm so flabbergasted by his reply that I almost drop my coffee. "You don't?"

"No, Paisley." He shifts abruptly to circle his shoulders like he's uncomfortable. "Marriage isn't always about love. It's about partnership. They had a partnership and an understanding. But is that why you upended your life? Because you learned that our grandparents didn't love each other?"

*Yes*. "No," I protest too much.

The way he's looking at me. He doesn't believe me.

"I just…" I squeeze my eyes shut, searching for the right words. I open my eyes again. "I think for me, TRANSPOT was an illusion that I talked myself into chasing because it made me feel closer to Grandfather. If I could keep the one thing that he believed in alive, then I could keep him alive as the greatest person God ever made. And everybody loved him, especially Grandmother."

"Pais? He lived in New York. She lived in Africa."

"But they would spend time together when they weren't working. You know, visit each other…?" That was more of a question than a statement.

"No, they didn't."

I'm shocked by how candid he's being about our grandparents' relationship. A weird sensation ripples through me, and my head feels heavy.

"Furthermore, TRANSPOT is not an illusion. We've made serious progress. I'm going to tell you this because I trust that you are loyal to our family first."

My lips are parted. I should stop him from saying whatever he's about to say. It's a ploy. It's his game plan. Max is luring me back into our secret world.

"My team has discovered NZNN light." There are only a few things in existence that can make Max smile that way, and discovering NZNN light is one of them. "Grandfather said the energy source exists, and it does." Max is reading my face as though it's the morning newspaper.

My heart is beating like crazy. I wish he'd never told me. NZNN light is negative-zero non-nomenclature light. If tweaked and harnessed the right way, the light source has the ability to take the molecules that are unseen in the air and solidify them. I can then use computer sourced nan-technology to make physical copies of any moving image. And I wish I didn't believe Max's claim. I wish he was a person who couldn't be believed. But Max has never lied to me and probably never will.

"How?" I say past my tight throat.

"Our team of physicists discovered it. But we need you to figure out how to program software that will allow us to capture the source and harness it."

I'm nodding as my insides cringe. My heart wants to grow feet and run far away from what he's not-so-directly asking me to do. I'm not ready. Especially after last Friday's hearing. I will not perpetuate this silly feud between the Lords and Groves. The time has come to bring it to an end.

An idea comes to me. "Ask me to work on TRANSPOT after you and Achilles figure out how to come to a satisfying settlement. For now, I'm pursuing other goals." I bite into my sandwich, hoping Max won't ask me what goals I'm pursuing. My plans are quite arbitrary. I'll finish decorating my house and then figure out how to get over Hercules for good. Some traveling might be involved. I should go see Grandmother in Botswana soon.

Max eyes me studiously as I chew without tasting. I haven't been enjoying the sandwich. I'm too anxious, although I don't let it show. I'm waiting to hear the million-dollar question.

Instead, Max stands and smooths the cloth of his pristine black dress pants. "I'll be in touch."

I'm going to burst. What a way to maintain the upper hand. I could insist he chooses the resolution

I suggested. Peace with the Lords over TRANSPOT is the only way I'll work on the project. But there's no need to hammer it home. Max understands it already.

"Okay," I say, keeping my cool as I hold up my barely eaten sandwich. "Thanks for coming by and bringing this."

"You're welcome." He nods graciously and heads to the door and then stops abruptly to face me. "But listen, Paisley. I can't promise you any sort of reconciliation with the Lords. You're attached to Hercules Lord at the moment. But he's getting married soon."

I'm stunned into silence as I watch him coolly turn away from me and saunter out of my apartment. *What does he mean by "getting married soon"?* I know Max better than I know anyone else on the face of the earth. He sounds like he knows something about Hercules that I don't know.

*But he can't know more than I do… can he?*

---

It's six o'clock on the dot when I enter the Blue Cherry on Eighth Street. When I looked into the mirror before heading out, the color had come back to my face, and the dark circles under my eyes had magically disappeared. I felt really good after my talk with Max, despite what he said before leaving. Max never makes flippant comments. I've been wondering if he knows something I don't. I should have called Hercules right away, but I was pressed for time. I'll call him as soon as I leave the bar.

Through a sea of mostly pretty female faces, my eyes locate my former assistant sitting at our favorite area at the bar. The reason there are so many women patrons is that the Blue Cherry only serves fruity and dessert-flavored cocktails. They use organic juices, natural flavoring, and alcohol, which indeed is a city girl's dream bar.

Ru frowns as I approach. When I'm closer she smiles as she slips off her stool. Then we hug like we're really going to miss each other.

"Oh, I already miss you," she whines.

"I already miss you too."

Finally, we release each other and take our seats. Ru has already ordered me a lemon cream pie drop. "It's on me," she says.

I thank her, and she goes right into telling me all about her morning. Apparently, my office was cleaned out when she arrived.

"First I wondered whether the carpet was being

shampooed. You know, like last time. But then your sourpuss brother walked into my space and announced that I was being reassigned to support a new executive."

I can imagine how insensitive Max's approach might have been. He's not one for exercising tact. "I'm so sorry, Ru."

Before I'm able to explain why he reassigned her, she grunts, throws a hand up, and says, "Then he asked, 'Aren't you and Paisley friends?' I said yes. And then he warned me not to discuss work matters with you. I mean, I got his drift. He didn't want me to say anything to you about what he was doing. He even told me exactly what to write in an email to you. I mean, really, Paisley, I know he's your brother and all, but he's got a serious God complex. What happened to him growing up? Why are you two so different?"

Ru looks like she's waiting to hear my answer. Truthfully, I have no clue about why Max and I are like night and day.

"I don't know why he and I are so different. But he stopped by my apartment this afternoon."

Ru appears taken aback. "He did?"

"Yes."

"After all that, he showed up at your place. Did he just want to act like an asshole?"

I chuckle uncomfortably as I ponder explaining my brother to her. She would need more insight into him to understand why he went about reassigning her the way he had. But Ru's right about Max's God complex. He wants to control how she and I discuss his actions.

That's simple enough to grasp, but I just say, "It's a family matter. And he knew I would quit, and that was why he reassigned you."

Her jaw drops. "You quit the company?"

"Yes. I did." I lift my cocktail to my lips. I feel great about my decision as I take my first sip. "Um," I hum with my eyes closed, relishing the flavor. "Delicious as always."

"Don't they make the best cocktails?" She takes a swig of her own lemon cream pie drop. "By the way, they reassigned me to Daniel Walton in the digital art department. I never met him—have you?"

I smile, reassuring her. "I have, and he's a good guy. You'll like him."

She puts a hand on my shoulder as she sighs with relief. "Thank you."

And just like that, discussion about Max and her horrible day ceases. Ru starts in on her favorite subject which is her boyfriend Rob and their latest adventures. I've met Rob a handful of times, and he strikes me as an energy sucker. Like, the topic of discussion has to be about him or nothing at all. I think that was why she made the best assistant ever. Ru, as beautiful and enigmatic as she is, prefers taking a back seat to a needier, more charismatic personality. She's reactive when it comes to Max, though, which surprises me. Rob is way worse. And apparently, he's selling his mother's Upper East Side townhouse and has saddled her with a bunch of tasks that he should pay somebody to do. She says Rob asked her to call various staging companies and make a list of prices.

I snort sarcastically and gaze off to the side. And that's when I notice someone staring at me. My head feels like it's taking a nosedive, and it's not from my cocktail.

"Oh my God," I whisper.

"What is it?" Ru asks.

"I'll be right back," I say, my eyes remaining pinned to Lauren, who's staring back at me.

---

Lauren and I have decided to take our conversation outside. It's noisy on the street as rush-hour traffic whizzes by in vehicles and on foot. But she and I can hear each other just fine, and that's all that matters.

Of course, she's a knockout. Her stretchy pink dress hugs all her curves, which are in the right places. The neckline dips low, showing off cleavage made by implants. I try not to imagine Hercules doing to her breasts what he's done to mine. But it's too late. I'm imagining it, and that upsets my stomach. And there's no love or like for me in the way her eyes regard me.

"Okay, why are you stalking me?" I ask curtly.

"If you weren't fucking my fiancé, I would have no need to be looking at you right now." She looks smug.

I could assure her that I have not had sex with Hercules after learning of his engagement to her, but I'm not going to. My mouth is tight. "What do you want?"

"Leave my fiancé alone."

"I'm not with Hercules. I'm out with a friend, enjoying a drink. But you're getting in the way of that."

Lauren looks like she wants to stomp me into

the concrete. "On Friday, our marriage will be finalized. I'm moving into his penthouse. I'll be giving birth to Hercules's babies, and that will be the end of you."

She sounds so certain, and that infuriates me even more. "He's not marrying you," I snap. "He assured me of that on many occasions."

"Oh, he's going to marry me. And because of the way you've been running around with him like the harlot that you are, we're doing it sooner than planned. So I thank you, and you can thank yourself for making sure he does what he's supposed to do, and that is marry me. And let me just show you so you can get the hell out of our lives." Her hands seem eager as she takes her cellphone out of her purse.

I've been stuck in a weird state of mind for several seconds. My head is light. All the ambient noise blaring around us is taking on a distant quality. It's as if I'm existing out of my body, as Lauren says she can prove it. My jaw is tight, and my lips are crushed as she shuffles through her cellphone. When she finds what she's looking for, she holds the screen up so I can see.

She has enlarged a portion of a contract that shows signatures and a claim of marriage between

Lauren and Hercules this upcoming Friday at noon. It's just as Hercules told me—his marriage to Lauren will not be performed in a ceremony. It will be made on paper.

"So leave him the hell alone, you bitch," Lauren hisses through clenched lips.

Her pretty face shows pure hatred. But I'm not intimidated by her. On the contrary, I'm jealous of her. I long to have what she has.

She's waiting. She wants to hear me say that I will leave them in peace. I look up, hoping to deny space for the tears that are rushing to my eyes. Whatever was going on with Hercules and me has already ended anyway. Now I know why he didn't call me last night—Achilles has punished him for sneaking off with me. And I bet Max knows what Lauren has just revealed to me. Now the final comment Max made to me this afternoon makes sense. It seems Hercules's brother and my brother can come together for a common cause—to make sure Hercules and I keep our distance from each other.

Even though I want to throttle Lauren for calling me a bitch, I say, "Okay."

One of her eyebrows shoots up like she's surprised I so easily acquiesced. My heart drops to my feet as I watch her stroll away. *She'll be having his children...* The thought makes my legs weak. I turn this way and that, looking for a seat or something to lean on.

I make it to Blue Cherry's brick wall and press my back against it. Tears stream down my face as a grave sense of loss takes hold of me and refuses to let go.

"Paisley?" Ru asks in a concerned voice.

Just hearing her makes me cry harder. My friend and former assistant throws her arms around me, and I bawl into her shoulder.

# The Aftermath

PAISLEY GROVE

Ru rides home with me in a cab. Fortunately, she calls Lake on the way back to my apartment, telling her what happened with Lauren and that I'll need a friend tonight. She would stay, but Rob is expecting her for dinner.

Lake is waiting for me in front of the building when the cab arrives. When we make it into the elevator, she tells me how awful it is that Hercules didn't have the guts to say something to me before Lauren spilled the beans. And just then, Treasure calls. I swear, my cousin is intuitively dialed in to me. Whenever I'm at a particularly low point in life, she calls.

With Treasure on speakerphone, we go to Lake's apartment, since Lake has already made dinner—wet red chili-mole beef burritos with margaritas. She had a taste for Mexican food tonight, and instead of ordering in, she tried a new recipe. Mason, who was supposed to join her, is stuck at the office. Instead of coming to her apartment when he leaves work, he's going home to sleep. He's been overly tired these days. So, basically, there's plenty of food for me.

"It's good you know now, though, Pais." Treasure yawns. "I think you should focus your energy on a sure thing from here on out."

"I agree," Lake says before putting a bite of burrito into her mouth.

I hang my neck. "Me too."

"Listen, lovelies, I have to go because the director just called me to the set. We're shooting my last scene of the day. Yay," she says in a weary voice.

"Are you getting enough sleep?" I ask.

"Absolutely not, but that's show business. And by the way, I think you're right. Max absolutely knew about Hercules marrying Lauren on Friday. He probably made a deal with Achilles to make it happen. You know it's totally him to do that, don't you? Okay, gotta go." Treasure hangs up. It's just like her to drop an atomic bomb before fleeing the scene.

Mouth open, I stare at Lake, remembering how Max showed up at my apartment, bringing me my favorite sandwich. "Oh no." I close my eyes and whisper, "How in the hell did I miss it? The sandwich. He feels guilty."

Lake's eyelids get stuck for a few seconds while she blinks as if she can hardly believe what she's being forced to process. "Wow, your brother's a real jerk."

My shoulders slump as I set my plate on my lap. I've momentarily lost my appetite. "Yeah." I sigh.

"And you know what, Paisley? Screw it. I'm going to insist Mason find a new best man. Because Hercules doesn't signify love. He signifies the opposite of love. And his front-stage presence at our wedding will taint us."

I'm confused about how to respond. That's awfully dramatic of her. Plus, I don't think Mason will change out his best man on my behalf. I'm a Grove, LTI's enemy.

I'm on the verge of telling Lake not to say anything to Mason when my cellphone rings. It's sitting on the coffee table. Lake and I crane our necks to see the name and number of the caller. I inhale sharply as we look at each other in surprise.

"It could be divine intervention," she suggests.

On the fourth ring, I answer, thinking maybe she's right. "Hi."

The caller is Clive, the lawyer. He asks if I'll have dinner with him tonight, but I say I'm already eating dinner, and then afterward, I'm just going to go to bed. I'm wiped.

Then he asks if I will go out with him tomorrow night. Even though I'd rather stay in and sulk, I say yes. Lake claps for me.

"That's how you get back on the horse, Pais," Lake says. "And I know Clive. He's a really good guy."

I narrow an eye. "Is that all? He's a good guy?" I remember that she described Hercules as *not boring*. "Is he boring?"

"No." She laughs softly and then she frowns. "I don't think so."

# Date Night

## PAISLEY GROVE

### WEDNESDAY NIGHT

The restaurant reminds me of a museum depicting the height of Roman opulence. After the waitress seats us at a table for two, Clive looks proud of himself for bringing me to this den of indulgence. All I can think is that Hercules would've never brought me here.

But to be fair, I don't think Hercules would be on my mind if Clive wasn't talking about him. He says he doesn't care for any of the Lord brothers, including Hercules, because they're cocky and don't believe the rules apply to them.

I want to say, "I'm sorry, but have you met my brother?" But I say nothing, believing a nonresponse will make him change the subject faster. It doesn't.

"And that girl Hercules is marrying—she's gorgeous. But I guess one isn't good enough. And they're dirty in business, so… you dodged a bullet."

The waiter sets the Gulf shrimp in front of me and the lamb chops in front of him. I dig in. While eating, I realize something. Clive has been doing most of the talking so far.

At this very moment, he's talking about his law firm and how fast he's moving up the ranks. Then he describes different cases he's argued and asks whether I've heard of any of them.

"Never heard of it," I reply to each.

Well, they're all apparently very important, which proves he has the juice to be GIT's sole counsel. Very quickly, Clive is reminding me why I rarely go on dates.

When is he going to ask me something about myself, especially since he likes me so much? He told me that on the drive to the restaurant. He likes me even though he doesn't know anything about me. But listening more than talking is the best tool to really get to know an individual—and I want to know if Clive has what it takes to replace Hercules.

So I don't remind him that a proper conversation involves two people and not just him.

"Oh, and I own a vineyard in Napa," he says. "April's the best time to go. I wouldn't mind flying out this weekend with you. That's if you have no plans."

His eyebrows are up. Finally, he's waiting for me to say something. And oddly, I have to think about it. It would be great to get away for the weekend that Hercules and Lauren will be officially married. But another thought comes to mind—a solution perhaps.

"Sorry, I'll be out of the country."

He raises his eyebrows higher. "Where are you going?" He sounds disappointed.

"Botswana. I'm going to stay with my grandmother for a while."

"Oh," he says, running a hand through his hair. He seems eager and anxious. I hope he's not going to say what I think he's going to say. "I've never been on a safari. It's on my bucket list, though. Maybe I'll join you. Or visit."

I sigh with a weary grunt. He said what I thought he was going to say. I hate being put in this position. Hercules's assessment of me was accurate.

I never beat around the bush, and I'm not going to start now.

I wipe my mouth with my cloth napkin and then place it next to my plate. I'm done eating. Listening to Clive go on and on for the better part of an hour has given me a headache. It's time for the table to be cleaned and prepared for the next set of daters, and ideally, their dinner will be more successful.

"Clive." I wait until I have his full attention. "You said you like me a lot. What exactly do you like about me?"

Confusion spreads over his face. He shifts in his chair and tugs at his collar. "What's not to like about you?"

I whip my head into a tilt. "Is that your way of saying you don't know exactly what you like about me?"

"You're beautiful, for one."

"And for two?"

He lifts one side of his mouth into a lopsided smile. "You smell good."

"Three?"

He throws up a hand like he's coming up with an answer before the clock runs out. "You're nice."

I've got to hand it to him—he knows how to

bullshit like a good lawyer. "Have you ever thought about being a politician?"

"Really? You're not the first person who's asked me that."

*Oh God, he didn't catch my sarcasm.* I look around. This restaurant is pretty hopping. The patrons are twice our age, but they're wealthy, gorgeous, and out to have a great night out. Maybe I would be having more fun here tonight if I'd come with Lake and Treasure.

"Paisley," he calls.

I snap my attention back to him. Gosh, I let my mind wander for too long. "Yes."

I see several things on his face. His lusty feline smile is one of them. Clive leans across the table, looking as if he's about to let me in on a secret. "You want to grab a room for the night?"

My shoulders are stiff as I pinch my back against my chair. I can't believe he asked me that. But I'm not infuriated or offended. Finally, he's talking my language, and my language is frankness.

Smirking, I bend forward so he can hear me clearly over the chatter. "No." I clutch my purse. I can't take this anymore. "Thank you for the dinner. Good night."

"Wait," he says, reaching out as if to stop me from leaving. "Where are you going?"

"Home"—I wave a hand, showing him the room—"but by all means, Clive, stay. Maybe you can coax one of the many lovely ladies here into joining you in your hotel room." In a loud whisper, I say, "Maybe you can tell them all about your vineyard in Napa too. Again, good night."

Striding through the restaurant, weaving through tables, I know better than to hail a cab right away. My guess is that it's going to take Clive about ten seconds to process what just happened between us. I certainly believe that he thinks going from dinner to his hotel room is a reasonable progression for the two of us. Once those ten seconds are up, though, he'll come looking for me and insist on driving me home, like a gentleman. And on the way, he'll apologize for his behavior without really comprehending why it was a problem. He'll just want another date so he can figure out a different way to get me in bed. It'll just be too awkward, and I don't want to keep turning him down.

So I hide out in the ladies' room. And while I'm in a stall, it finally hits me. He thinks I easily fall into bed with men because Hercules and I were caught tonguing by *Top Rag Mag* and had sex on the night of Lake and Mason's engagement party.

I groan into the palm of my hand. I have made all the wrong decisions since Hercules came back into my life. Starting tonight, I'll be making all the right decisions.

---

AFTER EXACTLY TEN MINUTES, I COME OUT OF THE stall, wash my hands, and then exit the ladies' room. My feet come to a grinding stop, and I'm shocked to see Clive standing with his hands in his pockets, gazing at me with a defenseless and contrite look on his face.

"Sorry," he says.

My lips part, but no words come out, not yet.

"I realize I came off like a jerk. My intention was not to take you upstairs to sleep with you."

The bathroom door opens. Since he said he was sorry, I let him close the distance between us as two ladies pass, eyeing us curiously.

"I wanted to get to know you better—that's all," he says, keeping his voice low.

I grunt bitterly. "How is taking me to your hotel room *getting to know me better* if sex isn't involved?"

"We could've shared a bottle of wine, talked, and then watched a movie or something. Listen…" He checks over his shoulder, to see who's chatting. Down the hallway walk a man and a woman, who appear to be lovers, heading in our direction. They pay scant attention to us as they pass. When we're alone again, I feel my armor dissolving. It takes guts to find me and face me so that we can talk it out.

"You're into Hercules Lord. I understand that. I was too eager. Talking about myself like a narcissist. I was trying too hard to convince you that I'm a better option, I think. But I know it's going to take some time for you to move past him. And, Paisley, I'm willing to wait. Because like I said, I like that you're beautiful and kind—gentle but strong and smart too. And you're graceful, Paisley, very grace-ful." Wearing the sincerest expression, Clive takes a step back to put a comfortable distance between us. "Please, will you let me take you home?"

# Everything Good

PAISLEY GROVE

*What's that noise? Where am I? Why can't I move?*

My arm stretches toward my chiming cellphone, proving that I can move. *What time is it?*

As soon as Clive showed me to the door, Lake texted and asked, *how was it?*

I responded: *It ended up okay. I'll tell you about it in the morning. Sleepy.*

She texted back: *Mason's here. Want to do lunch tomorrow?*

And I sent her a thumbs-up.

So surely this isn't Lake calling me so late—or early, depending on how one looks at it. But the chiming is annoying. I preferred the silence and being able to get much-needed sleep.

To stop the noise, I answer without looking to see who is calling. "Hello," I say tiredly.

"PG." Hercules's voice enters my ear like a sigh of relief.

I drag myself up to sit against the headboard. "Hercules?"

"Hey," he breathes.

"What do you want?" I sound cold, and that's deliberate. Yes—I have to work at it. And I hate that I have to work at it. I should be naturally angry with him. I should end our call right this second. But I can't. I need to hear what he has to say.

*Oh God, help me, but I think I'm a fool in love with him.*

Hercules sighs, and I can imagine him squeezing his temples the way he does when he's anguished. "I know I've been MIA," he whispers. There's a frog in his throat like he's getting sick or something.

But I'm ready to pounce. "By the way, Lauren showed me your marriage license yesterday. She'll officially be yours on Friday. Congratulations." *Ooh, it feels good to say that.*

"What?" he roars before I can say good night.

Every moment of my encounter with Lauren at the Blue Cherry comes gushing out of me. I have to catch my breath by the end of it.

"I can't believe her. She's desperate." Then he says with assurance, "I am never going to marry her, Paisley. I need you to believe that."

Eyes shut, I shake my head. I just don't understand what he means to do about it. Their marriage is already set in stone. "I don't know what to believe."

"Paisley, I've been MIA because I've been working on something, and I've gotten my days and nights turned upside down. But I've made some serious progress, and I want to let you in on it. Are you working tomorrow?"

*Oh, yeah, then there's the matter of my job.* "No," I say with a sigh. "I quit."

He's silent for several seconds. "Okay, then, let me swing by and pick you up at around seven in the morning. I want to take you somewhere, show you something."

I'm inclined to say no. I've lost faith in Hercules's claims of never marrying Lauren. Maybe not, though. Deep down inside, I have a glimmer of hope. I also have a question. I know how sexually attracted Hercules is to me, and of course, the feeling is mutual. But even though there's more than that between us, I refuse to give him one last roll in the hay before he skips off into happily never after with Lauren.

"Are you just trying to have sex with me?" I ask.

Hercules is silent for a few beats, but I maintain my resolve. I want to know the answer.

"No, Paisley, I am not trying to have sex with you. I promise, you will *want* to come with me. You'll want to see what I have to show you."

---

HOW IN THE WORLD COULD I HAVE FALLEN ASLEEP during those four hours between when Hercules called and seven in the morning, the time he was supposed to arrive? I just couldn't. I tried to make Hercules spill the beans, but he wouldn't do it.

"Not over the phone," he said.

Then I reminded him that we were supposed to hang out on Monday night, but he neglected to call me. Gosh, I sounded so sad.

Hercules explained that he'd mostly been awake for the better part of seventy-two hours, reading through the Lord Trust rules. "I really am sorry, PG. If it's any consolation, I've been missing the hell out of you. I wanted to call you early this morning. But I couldn't keep my eyes open. I meant to take a short nap, but I ended up crashing. I woke up, right before I called you. And I wish I could've prepared you for Lauren's bullshit. I didn't think she knew about the contract."

Okay, so his apology was pretty perfect. That was why I forgave him. However, I didn't tell him about my date with Clive. I guess I was ashamed to let him know how fast I was willing to move on to another man.

Hercules's SUV stops in front of my building. I check the time on my watch. He's five minutes early. And just like that, Clive has become a distant memory.

My heart stands at attention. I know what's coming next. My cellphone chimes as I hold it in my hand. Beaming, I answer it as I watch the Adonis known as Hercules Lord step out of the back seat. He's a glorious sight to behold—like a famous work of art.

"Hi," I whisper.

"Hi," he says back, gazing up at my picture window.

I wave at him just to see if he sees me. Hercules waves back. We're grinning at each other. My heart expands like a balloon in my chest.

"I'm on my way down," I sweetly say.

"I'll be waiting."

His voice releases butterflies in my chest. I end our call and race into my bedroom to examine myself in the standing mirror. I'm wearing faded-black skinny jeans, which I didn't realize I owned until I went searching for something that might be sexually appealing. *That's kind of a first for me. I want to arouse Hercules.* The tags were still on the jeans when I pulled them off the hanger. My blouse is white eyelet that tapers at the waist. Black booties are on my feet.

I look posh.

I approve.

I snatch my lightweight black duster sweater off the back of the sofa and race out of my apartment.

When I step out into the morning light and onto the sidewalk, I stop to regard the vision that is Hercules. He's staring at me with wonderment too. It's only been four days since we've seen each other, but it feels like it's been a lot longer.

"Wow," Hercules mouths as I exit the building and close the distance between us.

I simper bashfully and drop my eyes to the

concrete. I'm happy he approves. *Well done, Paisley Grove. Well done.*

He looks good too. He's wearing jeans too. They're light denim and they fit him perfectly—with ease. And he has on a dark blue T-shirt. On top of that, his cologne smells oh so delicious. I can never imagine him being with someone like Lauren. I can only picture him with someone like me.

Hercules's eyebrows gradually raise appreciatively. "You look stunning this morning, PG."

My smile lights me up from the inside out. I can't believe my reversal of fortune—and in a good way. The last two days were hellish, but now I feel stupidly incautious. I don't want to reprimand myself, though. I'm just going to go with it and let the chips fall where they may—at least for today.

"So do you," I say, still smiling.

Hercules and I remain stuck in each other's gaze. We should kiss. But kissing him now feels too premature. Given that he's going to be officially married in one day, I want to know what he has to show me first.

Finally, my smile wavers. Hercules must sense me faltering as he takes me by the hand. His grip is possessive. "We should get going. It'll take us a little less than an hour and a half to get there."

"Where are we going?" I ask, keeping my feet glued to the sidewalk. It's time he reveals something about what he has in store for us.

"Nova Scotia."

I yank my head back in surprise. "Canada?"

"Yes."

I spread my palm flat against my purse. "Thank goodness I keep my passport on me."

He wiggles his eyebrows. "Is that so?"

"Um-hmm." That sounds too syrupy, so I break eye contact so that my lady parts can settle down. They're too excited. So without further delay, I crawl into the back seat of Hercules's SUV.

James is behind the wheel. After we say good morning to each other, the privacy window rolls up. And now Hercules and I are all by ourselves.

---

SO FAR, WE'VE BEEN GETTING BY ON A LOT OF small talk. He's finishing up letting me know that he tried to talk Mason into getting himself checked on several occasions. It's just as Lake has claimed. Her fiancé is stubborn.

Now it's my turn, and I'm ready to ask what or who's in Canada. But before I can say anything,

Hercules asks me about Treasure. "Is she really engaged to Simon Linney?" He's watching me with intense focus.

I pause, wondering why he wants to know about Treasure's love life. "Why do you ask? Does Orion want to know?"

"No." Eyebrows ruffled—he's still waiting for me to answer his question.

"Unfortunately, yes."

His frown deepens. "You don't care for Simon Linney?"

I shrug indifferently. "I never met him, but his reputation precedes him. And then there's the matter of Treasure's picker, which is terrible."

Hercules tilts his head from one side to the other as though weighing my words. It looks as if he has something to say.

"What?" I ask.

"Nothing," he says in an unconvincing way.

I squish one eye thoughtfully. "You don't want to speak ill of your brother?"

Hercules belts a laugh. "No, that's not it."

I laugh too. "Then what?" I ask after we simmer down.

"It's something you said on our way to the Hamptons."

My eyes expand as I nervously try to chase down my words. I was nervous that night. I could've said anything. "What did I say?"

"You said she's been cut off, financially?"

Air cools my eyes as they expand. "I did?"

Eyes dancing around my face, Hercules chuckles. "It's okay, PG. Her secret is safe with me."

I press my hand on my chest as I sigh with relief. "Good because she'll kill me if she knew I told Orion's brother." I drop my hand and relax a bit more. "But you still haven't told me why you care about Treasure's finances."

Hercules winks at me. "In due time, PG—in due time."

My mouth is caught open. All the mystery behind our trip and how it applies to Treasure is driving me crazy. But Hercules takes me by the hand and weaves his large fingers between mine. I forgot what I was thinking as our eye contact deepens. We're looking at each other longer than we should. Then, my eyes fall to his lips, and I gulp. His lips are so scrumptiously swollen. He has a delicious mouth, perfect for kissing. My sex is drumming. My pulse is racing. I want out of my clothes. I want him inside me, now.

But fortunately, we arrive at the airport before

anything can happen. There's so much room in the back seat of his SUV. I'm wearing my black lace panties and on purpose. *Scheming Paisley.* Right now, the crotch is soaking wet.

---

ON HERCULES'S PRIVATE AIRPLANE, I'M LESS flustered by being near him. Before boarding, he assured me more than once that his inquiry about Treasure will make sense soon. He asked me to please go with the flow. It was hard to yield, but I said I would. We sit across from each other. The large aircraft has six big armchairs on a platform in the middle of the cabin and the same sort of chairs along the sides. Hercules says there's a bedroom on board with a full bath. He even offers me a tour. But I graciously decline. No way do I want to see a bed on his airplane. I recall Lake's birthday cake analogy, and that bed is birthday cake.

Right now, I'm avoiding looking at my traveling companion. Maybe I should have sat beside him. My gaze betrays me and sneaks a peek at him. But I quickly shift my eyes down to the cappuccino in front of me. What a face he has—extremely handsome. However, I realize that instead of beating back my desire for Hercules, I should be more focused on figuring out what's behind this trip we're taking. Keeping my mind on that might be the best way to stave off lust.

"So, Hercules," I ask, lifting my cappuccino to my mouth. We're not being served a full breakfast because Hercules said we were going to eat at our destination. "Where are you taking me?"

Hercules sits very still for several seconds. He seems to be considering my question. "I want to ask you something."

I set my cappuccino back down. "Okay."

"Why haven't you ever asked me about my grandfather?"

His question makes me open my eyes wider. I didn't expect him to ask me that. "I don't know," I say. But Hercules seems to know me well enough to remain quiet as my thoughts take me through several iterations of the truth. I start over again. "Maybe I never asked because your grandfather would remind me of my grandfather." I twist my lips thoughtfully because there's more. "Also, I don't think I'll be able to stand it if you say anything negative about my grandfather in defense of your grandfather."

I draw my shoulders back as I inhale audibly

and then release my breath. It feels good to finally admit that. Hercules observes me in silence, leaving me to wonder if I should have kept that nugget of truth to myself.

"I want to show you something," he finally says.

My head feels floaty as I nod. He does something on his phone and then holds it out to me, and I take it. It takes me a minute to figure out what I'm looking at. It's an oil painting of some sort. The entire canvas isn't in view, though—just the bottom of it. I make out yellow tulips in a garden. Blades of grass. Hints of sky. The painting isn't as polished as Lake's works of art. Lake really is a phenomenal artist. But the piece in Hercules's phone does have a professional-looking signature.

I read the cursive strokes. My jaw drops. "No way," I whisper, feeling like all my breath has left my body.

"Yes," Hercules says, nodding. "Yes, babe."

# Who Is Garnet?

### HERCULES LORD

The deal is, Paisley looks and smells pretty tempting today. I'm trying to exercise self-control. Frankly, I don't understand why she's holding out. When the Earth collides with the sun, that will be the day I marry Lauren Mueller. I said that from the beginning and meant it.

Last night, after I hung up with Paisley, I finally rang Lauren back. She actually bragged about ruining my relationship with Paisley at the bar. She said she was prepared to lie and say I had fucked her, too, if that was what it would take to be rid of Paisley for good.

The woman's crazy. It's the sort of streak that runs through Lord women.

"Is that so?" I said, remaining cool, calm, and collected. I was finally ready to show my hand.

"Yes," she hissed like the snake that she was.

"Here's the thing, Lauren. When your great-grandfather—the one with all the money—was as misogynistic as ours was, you have to be very careful. I wouldn't call him a prick, though. He was just a man of his era." Then I sent her the video of her blowing Orion in the hot tub.

I could hear her listening to it because I captured the sound of water shifting, Orion sucking air, Lauren sucking cock, and me whispering, "I've got you. I've got you where I want you." The next thing I knew, Lauren had ended the call without another word.

She's been handled. I'll send the video to Achilles and my mother after I learn how this day will end. The power's in my hands now. If I send the same video to the board of the Lord Trust, Lauren will be ineligible to marry me. As a result, we will not receive the benefit for keeping it in the family. She's no longer "pure." What a load of crap. But still, the rules are what they are. And I don't care about the money. As I said, I have a hand to play. If I play that hand right, we will never have to demean ourselves to stay wealthy.

Paisley is still looking at me with shock. Her lips are parted and form an O. I want to suck them into my mouth, taste them. She's a sensual kisser.

"Wait. Are you saying that your grandfather is Garnet?" she finally asks.

I swallow and make room for my boner in my pants. "I think so." Actually, I know he is. I've thought about it a lot. It makes sense that a woman came between our grandfathers, which caused the rift between them.

Eyes closed like she wants to avoid seeing the truth, PG shakes her head. "Did you mention the letters to your grandfather?" she whispers, her voice thick with worry.

"No."

Her eyebrows ruffle. If she's relieved by my answer, I can't tell. She sure isn't happy about it.

"Are you going to tell him?"

I shake my head slowly. "I'll leave that up to you."

———

PG SAYS SHE WANTS TO REST HER EYES, AND I DON'T object. I study every angle, line, and curve of her beautiful face as she closes her eyes to think. I know that's what she's doing. Like me, she's too wired to sleep.

The time has come. This is it. After all the years we've been wanting to know how the feud began between our families, we will now have the answer. For the longest time, I thought the bad blood resulted from TRANSPOT. But that's not it.

PG's eyebrows furrow just a bit. She must be tortured by her thoughts. She's always been a thinker. It's one of the many reasons why she's never left my thoughts. I always wanted to know what's going on inside her head. There aren't many people like her in the world. I know this because I've traveled to a lot of places, and met a lot of people. Her brain must work nonstop as she ponders everything she sees as if it's a thing to be taken apart, studied, and then put back together differently.

One day, I'll tell her about that New Year's Eve night when I made love to her. I was supposed to get together with a girl I met two days before. I forget her name—Mandy or Andy— but she'd come up to me at a coffee shop downtown and asked for my number. I had to admit, her approach was bold. Also, she was pretty hot, but she didn't arouse me the way PG does.

"I can be your New Year's Eve date and kiss you when the clock strikes twelve," she'd said, all smiles and batting her eyelashes. "Like Cinderella."

I said, "Okay," and then gave her the address to the party I planned to attend.

The girl must have been playing coy or something, planning to arrive just before midnight. But by eleven o'clock, I'd run into PG at the bar.

*Goodness, that intense feeling.* I hadn't experienced it since the first time I saw her in high school. I bet she doesn't know she was the talk of the town before she even arrived at our school. Another Grove would be attending DMA. That meant the students were sharpening their swords, getting ready to take her down.

I could've stopped the campaign against her before the school year started, but—I'm embarrassed to admit—I was okay with another Grove biting the dust. Until I laid eyes on Paisley. I could tell that half the male student body was pretending that they weren't infatuated by her too.

Paisley Grove was a creature of pure perfection, a male's fantasy, a sexy vision in nerd garb. One look was all it took. I used to picture her whenever I beat off. I was obsessed. And then I got to know her, and I fell for her. I knew we could never be with each other, though. I couldn't stick my cock into her either. Well, I could've if I tried. But I didn't want to tarnish anything genuine that could ever happen between us. I guess deep down I knew we would be like this—on an airplane together and clearly in love.

But when I saw her the night of the New Year's Eve party, we were no longer in high school. College was almost done. Paisley Grove had breasts, the best ass a man could grab, and the face of an angel. Forget being reverent. I had to have her.

We talked for a while, but my boy hormones were on sensory overload. I can't remember what we talked about. She said something about her classes and putting homework off. We didn't have time for too much small talk, though. I knew Mandy or Andy would soon arrive, and I'd chosen to kiss PG when midnight struck. No—I wanted to be inside her. So I asked her back to my place. And the rest is history.

*But she was a virgin, huh?*

She was tight. Wet. I fought like hell to hold on. I wanted to make her think I had the stamina of a bull. Her supple thighs against me. Her even softer body beneath me. I came early. And I came hard.

"PG," I say, the words escaping me before I can

stop them. Her eyes open wide. They're not tired at all. I didn't think they would be.

I unbuckle my seatbelt. She doesn't miss a beat as I rise to my feet and take a step to stand in front of her. The depth of our contact makes my cock grow and grow and…

I bend down and unbuckle her seatbelt. When she's free of the strap, I take her by both hands and guide her to her feet. I'm glad that she's easily following my lead.

Her head is tilted back, and her mouth is ready for me to slip her some tongue. Her breaths blow across my face, warm, soft, and delicious.

And then I slide my tongue across her pouty bottom lip. "Umm…"

# A Pearl of a Surprise

## PAISLEY GROVE

Hercules's lips brush against mine, testing the waters. His intense eyes draw me into his soul as his tongue cautiously slips into my mouth. My eyelids flutter closed as sheer gratification rises through me.

I am like putty in Hercules's strong arms. My legs are like jelly. His tongue never tasted and felt so delicious—minty, warm, and honeyed.

Then, his hands grips my ass and presses me against his cock. He's overly ready to be inside me. All I can think about is that "birthday cake." *Maybe we should get it over with already.*

His mouth trails wet warm kisses down the side of my neck as one hand finds its way under my blouse and bra. I gasp as he softly squeezes the round of my breast and then pinches my nipple.

"I need it, baby," he sighs.

Then the flight attendant clears her throat.

I'm dizzy, and my eyelids are hooded as I turn toward the woman with the long dark hair. Hercules faces her too. She looks flustered when she says we're preparing for landing.

He nods briskly, his way of thanking her. She turns and escapes faster than a roadrunner. Then Hercules and I stare into each other's eyes again. Unfortunately, my lust for him hasn't been quelled, and I don't think his has either.

"Thank you for letting me do that," Hercules whispers, his voice thick with desire.

I would say that he's welcome, but I don't feel that's the appropriate response. I do want to thank him for just going for it and kissing me. It may have very well been our last kiss ever.

It takes a while for Hercules and me to let go of each other. But slowly, his hands abandon my body, and then his firm front side, including his manhood, is no longer against me. We watch each other as the pilot announces that we will be touching down in seven minutes. I feel as if my lips are mimicking his barely perceptible smile. Our thoughts might be the same too. I'm wondering what this thing between us is. I used to have a crush on Michael Rosa in third grade. His dark hair and brown eyes were insanely gorgeous. I used to make out with my pillow, pretending it was him. But today, I can't really picture Michael's face or what he might look like at twenty-nine or thirty. There were also Norman Jones, Kwan Lee, and Sean Pratt, all beautiful boy crushes, each having mysterious, quiet demeanors and quick eyes that saw what no one else was looking at. A lot like Hercules. But still, I regard what I felt for them with embarrassment. I was a young girl. I knew nothing about those boys. Their quietness could've been fear. Life isn't easy for most kids.

However, when I first saw Hercules, I knew I felt something different. The way we would constantly stare at each other was different. No matter where we were, if we were in the same vicinity, his eyes would find mine and mine would find his.

I recall the time I went to his rowing match. He was the boy in the front of the canoe, facing the guy who sat opposite the rest of the team. I later learned that Hercules was the "stroke."

The race was pulse-pounding. It looked as if DMA would lose by a hair, but they came back strong for a decisive victory. He never saw me behind three layers of spectators who were jumping up and down, hugging and cheering. Our school-mates who had seen me regarded me snidely as if to ask, "What's she doing here?" I didn't stay long after that. I went back to the car, where Greg, our driver, was parked and waiting for me.

Then Mr. Northam put us on that project together. Hercules and I designed an app for his crew team that helped them time each team member's strokes for maximum benefit, which resulted in DMA winning the championship—first for the region, then for the state, and then for the world. The rowing team still uses the app today. The school owns the intellectual property. I never let my family know Hercules and I were working on a class project together. If I'd done that, they prob-ably would have insisted that Mr. Northam assign me a new partner, and I didn't want that to happen.

"Remember that app we made in Mr. Northam's class?" I ask as the airplane drops lower.

Every part of Hercules's face is smiling—his lips, cheeks, and eyes. "Very much so."

"Did you ever mention our project to your family?"

Hercules lifts his eyebrow. "Just one person."

"Oh," I say, bracing myself as the wheels of the airplane hit the runway.

"Garnet handled the whole deal with the school."

It takes me a moment to process what he just said. *Garnet?*

I look at him incredulously. "Your grandfather?"

Nodding, Hercules says, "He made sure the school couldn't monetize our software and that either you or I only—not GIT or LTI—could buy back our rights and ownership from the school district whenever we wanted."

I'm speechless. *Why would Hercules's grandfather do anything for Gregory's granddaughter?*

"And you never bought the rights back?" I ask. "Because the script we made had some great parts to it. My skills in high school were pretty advanced." I grin, proud of myself.

Smiling, Hercules seems to consider what I asked. "I couldn't have done it without your consent. Plus, I didn't even know how the hell you did it! You were the brains, PG."

I leer at him shamelessly. I am throbbing downtown, and I don't care. "But you were the brawn."

We both say something about making money, and then we laugh. But actually, building on the app isn't such a bad idea.

---

WE'VE LANDED AND HAVE TAKEN A SHORT RIDE TO where a speedboat is docked. In the car, I asked Hercules about his father.

"We're not in touch," he said gruffly.

Ever since then, it's been sort of weird between us. But now we're on the boat, and with the engine roaring, we can't talk about it. Hercules handles the speedboat expertly. I can't keep my eyes off him as we glide against the dark water on our way to a private island. I bet Hercules can do anything. Well, except code. I laugh to myself at my little inside joke. He turns in time enough to see me smiling, which must be infectious because finally, he smiles too.

"What?" he bellows above the rumbling engine and splattering ocean.

"You look sexy driving a boat—that's all."

He drops his head back to roar with laughter and then booms, "Good!"

And I don't look away from him. I gawk shamelessly. I can do that now that we aren't in high school anymore, and he knows that I have feelings for him. He even knows that he's my first cock ever. So I get to stare at him if I want.

---

SOON, LARGE EVERGREENS AND PLUSH GRASS surrounding a mansion made of stone grace the scene. The abode looks like something rich hobbits would live in. Suddenly, I'm nervous. So, this is where Hercules Lord's grandfather has been all these years—on a private island off the coast of Nova Scotia. Also, he might have been in love with my grandmother.

When we make it to the plank, I'm sick to my stomach. Hercules instructs me to stay seated until he ties off the boat. I turn to stare at the house. It's chillier in Nova Scotia than in New York. I'm shivering, but it's more from my nerves than the cold.

"You ready?" Hercules asks with an assuring smile. He holds his hand out, and I try to put on a brave face as I let him help me out of the boat.

When we're standing on the dock, Hercules guides me in for a hug. "You're shaking." He quickly takes off his jacket and drapes it around my shoulders.

"I'm nervous too," I admit.

Hercules embraces me tighter, my face pressed against the soft sweater over his hard chest.

"You asked me about my father," he says, approaching the topic cautiously.

"Yes," I whisper.

"My father was never built for all of this. He could've lived without all the money from the start. He runs a cabana bar in Tahiti, and he's happy doing that." Hercules grows silent, but he's still holding me tight. "I've been mad at him for years. But you know, I think, up until you asked about him, I just let it go." He tilts back so I can see his face. "If I can do whatever it takes to follow my heart, then I can't deny my father the same opportunity."

Our eye contact deepens. I want to tell him that he's come to a beautiful conclusion about his father —but I can't stop biting down on my back teeth to keep my teeth from clattering. I smile tightly and nod instead.

"Everything's going to be fine, PG." His voice is gentle and reassuring. I love his tone.

But still, I glance nervously at the house. "Does he know we're coming?" I strain to whisper.

After a long pause, Hercules says, "No."

My eyes expand. "Why not?"

Hercules presses his lips together, looking wary. "Because I don't want to give him time to think about how he's going to answer our questions."

"But how do you know he's home?"

"He's home, PG. My grandfather's a creature of habit. In a few minutes, Bartleby, the baker, will arrive. Then Geneva, the cook, will put breakfast on the table. And we'll join him."

I lean farther away from Hercules to get a better view of his face. I want to see if he's gone mad. "We're crashing your grandfather's breakfast?"

Hercules's shrug doesn't do much to settle my nerves. "I wouldn't call it that."

But... his lips are on mine, and I let him kiss me gently. I must say, this settles me. He ends our kiss, and my lips feel the abandonment.

"Now, let's go."

"Wait," I quickly say.

He looks concerned. "What is it?"

"What you said about your father, the conclusion you drew…"

"Yeah."

"It's very beautiful."

Even though it's cold and I'm still shivering, we smile faintly at each other. Hercules comes in for another soft kiss. The passion in my chest wants to explode as I taste his mouth, but my nerves won't let it. Our lips part, and he asks if I'm ready. My head feels spasmodic when I nod. Then Hercules takes my hand and leads me to the house.

---

Before we make it to the porch, I notice smoke rising into the sky. It wasn't there when we docked. His grandfather must have just made a fire. So he is home.

The grass is emerald green. What a beautiful home Mr. Hugo Lord has. That's his name. I remember that. I love how he lives. I would live this way, too, if I could.

"You okay?" Hercules asks as we walk up the steps to the wraparound porch.

I nod stiffly. My body won't let go of its nervousness, but that doesn't mean I don't feel safe and protected next to the man I love. Hercules rings the doorbell, knocks once, and then takes a key out of his pants pocket and uses it to open the lock.

I gasp and give him a look of disbelief. The "really?" eyes.

Hercules holds the door open for me to enter first. "PG, I didn't know you were such a scaredy-cat."

My feet are glued to the porch, even though Hercules was also right about his grandfather having breakfast ready at this hour. I smell the food saturating the air, and the scent reminds me that I'm starving. "What if your grandfather has a big gun with the barrel aimed in our direction, ready to fire at intruders?"

Hercules laughs. "That's quite a picture you've painted. My grandfather doesn't own a gun. This is Canada." He winks as he points his head at the grand foyer. "Babe, my grandfather's house is the safest place on Earth. Now, ladies first."

I squish my face, frowning. "How about gentlemen first in this case?"

Hercules takes my hand, enfolding his fingers with mine. Then I'm against him, and his lips are on mine. But even a sensual kiss isn't enough to ease my worry.

"How about we go in together?" he whispers, his breath hot on my mouth.

A woman gasps loudly. Hercules and I quickly turn in her direction. Now I gasp. I close my eyes tight and then open them again. Nope, she's still standing there.

"Paisley," the woman says, and her voice is too familiar. Yes, it's her.

"Grandmother?"

# Answers

## HERCULES LORD

PG gapes at me as if I should know the answer to why her grandmother is standing in front of us, wearing a pink robe. *Does she live here?* If not, then she sure has made herself at home. I'm just as shocked as she is to see her grandmother inside my grandfather's house.

"Oh dear," Paisley's grandmother says. Her face is flushed as she pinches her top lip. Every so often, I catch Paisley doing the same thing.

"What are you doing here?" Paisley screeches.

Mouth caught open, her grandmother's confused eyes shift from Paisley to me and then back to Paisley.

"What is it, hon?" my grandfather calls and

then enters the foyer as if he hasn't a care in the world. He's wearing a plaid robe and pajama bottoms. He looks flabbergasted when he sees me. "Hercules?"

"Yeah," I say, my mind racing, still putting the pieces together. Then I realize Paisley and I have stumbled into a favorable predicament.

---

AFTER BARTLEBY DELIVERS THE BREAD AND GENEVA serves breakfast, Paisley and I sit at the table with our grandparents. Bartleby's biscuits with blueberry jam and strawberry preserves, light and fluffy scrambled eggs, home fries, and bacon are before us. Paisley, who I know was hungry before, hasn't touched a thing. I understand why she isn't eating because I, too, have lost my appetite. I need my grandfather to explain why Leslie Grove is at the table with us and not at a wildlife preserve on the other side of the world.

My grandfather, who has the vitality of a man almost half his age, sits stiffly in his chair. I understand that he's not happy to see me. If I were in his shoes, I wouldn't be happy to see me either.

"You should've called, Hercules," he grumbles.

I smile smugly. "I'm sure you would've answered the door if I had."

My grandfather scowls. He didn't like my response. I'm not used to speaking to him that way, but the situation we found them in reeks of deception, one that has probably been going on for years.

"Okay. You said you'll explain once we were seated. Now, explain yourselves, please," Paisley says, cutting to the chase. Her face is bloodless. I'm worried about her—especially after how she broke down at Friday's hearing.

Leslie extends an arm toward Paisley. Her limb isn't long enough to reach her, though. Our grandparents pass each other a look, and then Paisley and I exchange a similar leery glance. But Paisley… she looks exhausted.

"Well…" Leslie starts and then sits taller. "Hugo and I are together."

"I can see that," Paisley retorts briskly and then squeezes her eyes closed. When she opens them, she looks at my grandfather. "Are you Garnet?"

All the blood seems to drain from Hugo's face. "What do you know about Garnet?"

"I found letters from Garnet to you, Grandmother. Have the two of you been lovers since before…?" Paisley frowns as if her thoughts sting.

I'm about to call out to her and suggest we go for a walk, take a break, and get some crisp, cool air before we continue chomping at this elephant one bite at a time.

But then in a small voice that's almost as soft as a breeze, Leslie says, "Yes."

Paisley goes stiff, and so do I.

"If you're asking whether I was in love with Hugo before I married Charles, then the answer is yes."

Paisley turns to look at me. But it's as if she's seeing right through me before she turns her ire back on her grandmother. "Then why did you even marry him?"

"Because…" Leslie starts but then sits up straight as though she's considering how she feels about answering to her granddaughter.

"Leslie married Charles because I couldn't be with her."

Suddenly, I'm struck by illumination and ask, "Was Grandmother your cousin?"

My grandfather nods briskly.

"Fifth or sixth?"

"Fifth."

I sneer, and I shake my head.

"So you never loved Grandfather?" Paisley asks.

Her face is anguished.

"Does it matter?" Leslie replies.

"Yes!" she shrieks, throttling her hands back and forth.

We all go stiff. I've never seen PG this way.

"Let's remain calm," my grandfather interjects. I can tell that he doesn't like to hear Paisley speak to her grandmother that way. He never would have let me get away with that tone.

"Paisley?" I say.

She looks at me with helpless eyes. But I know she's okay when she attempts a smile.

"Sweetheart, you've always been intuitive. Therefore, I know you'll understand when I say that my relationship with Charles was my relationship with Charles. It had nothing to do with you."

Her frown deepening, Paisley says, "But..." She presses back against her chair. Her thoughts must have stopped her from speaking.

Finally, Leslie sighs. She's beautiful, with her heart-shaped face and eyes as gray as a cat's. "Charles and I didn't get married under the most blissful circumstances. He was in love with me, but I was in love with another man."

"And I was in love with her. Very much so," my grandfather says right before he and Leslie look at each other in a similar way to how Paisley and I often find ourselves gazing at each other.

There's no need to ask my grandfather if he ever loved Penelope, my grandmother. They never showed us that they loved each other. Neither did my mother and father. And oddly, I'm finding myself a bit annoyed with Paisley for not understanding that life and partnership aren't always made of fairy-tale plots.

My grandfather goes on to explain that he and Charles were business partners, and he was the one who introduced Charles to Leslie. For Charles, it was love at first sight.

"I wasn't free to marry her, but that didn't give Charles the right to get involved with her. We were friends and business partners. There was a line, and he crossed it."

When I turn to Paisley, she's already looking at me. Rubbing the side of her neck, Paisley says, "It's hard to believe that a love triangle wreaked so much havoc on our families."

"I'll take responsibility for the rift between our families," Hugo says. "I was bitter."

"And I married Charles because I was young and angry." Leslie shakes her head as if she finds her younger self's choices disappointing. "But I'm glad I married Charles because I have Xander and Leo, you and Treasure and Lynx. Sometimes beauty can arise from heartbreak."

I'm choked up by Leslie's words. Paisley nods stiffly.

"Did you read the letters?" Hugo asks, peering intensely at Paisley.

After staring into his eyes for several beats, Paisley swallows audibly and then says, "Every single one of them—multiple times."

My grandfather and Paisley watch each other. It's as though she sees his carefully concealed panic —and he knows that she knows why he's panicking.

"What is it?" I blurt.

Paisley shoots me a wide-eyed glance. Then she inhales deeply, and when she exhales, it's as if all the tension she's carried since we took our seats leaves her. She turns to her grandmother. "Garnet, who's Mr. Lord, was willing to run away with you, Grandmother," she says, her voice breaking. She sniffs. "But his letters took on an interesting tone. It sounded as though you were answering him. But I knew it wasn't you." Tears are rolling out of Paisley's eyes. She uses the cloth napkin to wipe them away.

I scoot my chair close to hers and put my arm

around her, and she rests her soft cheek on my chest. I want to kiss her on top of her head, but my grandfather appears awed by how intimate I'm being with Paisley. He knows I'm supposed to marry Lauren. His house on the private island and my family's opulent lifestyle depend on it.

My grandfather coughs to clear his throat. Then he focuses solely on Leslie. "I figured out Charles had been intercepting my letters when he showed up at the chapel instead of you."

"What?" she asks, looking and sounding shocked.

Paisley sits up on her own again. "By the tone of the later letters, I figured out Grandfather had been answering Garnet on your behalf."

However, I don't think Leslie is listening to her. She's staring at my grandfather in awe. He's watching her in the same way. I almost feel like Paisley and I should leave and give them some time to talk it out.

"You were going to give up the money and obligation and marry me?" Leslie tightly whispers.

"Yes," Hugo says, shaking his head fervently. I can see by the look on his face that he would do anything for Leslie Grove, then and now.

Every person at the table is still. The silence isn't

awkward either. It's needed. I know I shouldn't be the first to say something, and neither should Paisley.

"I guess the bright side is," Leslie says with a smile, "if we'd thrown caution to the wind and followed our hearts, then the two of you wouldn't be here, and clearly, you're in love."

The tension-filled silence could be sliced with a carving knife. We are all aware that for a Grove and a Lord, being in love isn't easy.

---

WE HAVE BREAKFAST BEFORE IT CAN GET ANY colder. Paisley's appetite seems to be back, and I'm glad she's eating well. She and I are eating in silence as my grandfather tells us about his relationship with Charles Gregory Grove. He says Charles, or Charlie, came to him, hoping he would invest in TRANSPOT. Charlie had heard that my grandfather funded ambitious projects like his.

"Charlie and I became good friends," Hugo says, with his eyes on Paisley as if he really wants her to know that.

She nods, chewing.

Then my grandfather scrapes his fingers down

the side of his face, a sign that he's experiencing discomfort. "Business and relationships got the best of us. I can't say I regret how I handled the past because, as Leslie said, if I'd done it differently, then I wouldn't have you, Hercules, and Leslie wouldn't have you, Paisley." My grandfather puts an elbow on the table and leans on it, angling himself toward me. "You're in the same position I found myself in many years ago, aren't you?"

My throat is tight, and my head is taking a nosedive. "Yeah," I sigh.

"Well, you have my blessing to marry who you love and only who you love. The money isn't worth the misery."

"I know. But I have a solution."

Hugo folds his arms. "You do?"

I swallow hard. This is it. I wasn't going to make this the moment, but no other time feels better for it than the present.

"The marriage will be finalized on Friday if I'm not already married before then." I turn slowly to Paisley. Her fork of scrambled stalls in front of her sexy lips, and very slowly, her eyes expand as she understands what I'm alluding to.

# Put Love First

PAISLEY GROVE

"**I**f you marry me, that will nullify the contract," Hercules says. His face the picture of unrestrained bliss. I've never seen him look so lit up, so unencumbered.

My mouth is caught open. I must look as happy as he does because along with being unable to believe Hercules Lord has asked me to marry him, I feel the way he looks.

But then, as he studies me, his face shifts through several contortions. "You don't have to marry me, of course. I have another option, but I prefer this one."

"No," I finally say in a tight voice as tears roll freely down my face. But then I flinch, panicking because I don't want him to misunderstand me. "I mean, yes, I'll marry you. Yes, yes, yes!"

We're on our feet. I'm in his arms. I'm experiencing a head-spinning kiss as he turns me in circles.

*Holy moly. He just proposed, and I said yes. Holy moly.* Our lips separate so we can gaze into each other's eyes.

Finally, Hercules forces his glassy eyes off mine to regard my grandmother. "Will that be okay with you, Mrs. Grove?"

My grandmother reaches out to massage Hugo on his shoulder. Looking blissfully elated, she says, "Yes. You have my blessing."

---

AFTER BREAKFAST, HERCULES AND I COULDN'T STAY on the island. We wanted to—there was a bedroom with our name on it at the rear of the house, facing the ocean. Hugo wanted to hear more about Hercules's next plan, but Hercules told him he wanted to keep it to himself until the outcome was set in stone. He did, however, say that it had to do with a loophole in trust rules. And then he spouted off a bunch of numbers and some legal jargon. If I wasn't still reeling from being out-of-this-world thrilled about becoming Mrs. Hercules Lord, I would've committed those numbers to memory.

However, Hercules and I have set our plans in motion. Today, we'll get married. Tomorrow, we'll fly back to Nova Scotia and spend the first part of our honeymoon with our grandparents before Hugo and Leslie visit their children to explain their relationship. Oddly, Hercules's father, Christopher, already knows about them.

Now we're on Hercules's private airplane. I'm not stalling anymore. I am his, and he can have me. I've allowed Hercules to lead me to his private bedroom. We're heading to Las Vegas, Nevada. New York would have been the easiest town to marry in, but it's also the riskiest.

On the car ride to the airport, Hercules sent a series of messages from his cellphone, during which he asked me for all the information needed to file for a marriage license. After we boarded, he said, "We should be all set with a license as soon as the airplane touches down in Nevada."

We're at the foot of the bed in the airplane, holding hands, our fingers tightly interwoven. The hair on my arms stands at attention. So do my nipples. And my sex, well… the throbbing between my legs is nothing short of extreme.

But we are gazing into each other's eyes. All of me, from head to feet, is experiencing sensory overload. My lips want his, but something is stopping me. And so I say what's on my mind.

"I went on a date with Clive last night." The sentence comes pouring out of my mouth like a forced confession.

Hercules grunts as he appears to thoughtfully consider what I just said. Stroking his chin, he says, "That lucky dog. Where did he take you?"

"The St. Regis."

He grunts judgmentally as he wraps me up, and we scoot to the head of the bed. "I'm not surprised. I never would've taken you there."

I'm on my back. He is stretched out on his side, slowly unbuttoning my blouse.

"I know," I sigh. My body aches for his hands on my skin.

"I would've just taken you to the real Rome."

My lips stretch into a naughty little feline smile. "That was exactly what I thought."

I chuckle right before his lips land on mine. His tongue tastes divine. He tastes different now that he's going to be my husband. I luxuriate in what's to come as he finishes unbuttoning my blouse.

Eager to speed up the pace, I take his shirt by the hem, and for a second, we lose lip contact so that I can get it up and over his head. He frees my breasts from my bra. Tossing my head back, I inhale a cold drink of air as my nipple experiences his warm, wet mouth.

"Mr. Lord, you have an important message," a woman's voice says through a speaker attached to the wall.

With my nipple cooling from the wetness and from the abandonment of his warm mouth, I can feel Hercules's breath upon the tip as he mutters a string of curse words.

"I'll be right back. Get naked," he says before rushing out of the bedroom.

---

I'VE BEEN NAKED FOR WHAT FEELS LIKE A MIGHTY long time. I'm underneath the luxurious duvet. My body is warm. As I stare at the ceiling, my eyelids are getting heavier by the second. Hercules has been gone for more than twenty minutes. I yawn and close my eyes and contemplate getting dressed and going out to see what's going on. But I can't move. I'm too comfortable, and so very tired.

Then I turn onto my side. It has been a jam-packed morning following a late night. And after Hercules called to tell me that he had this day planned for us, I couldn't get back to sleep. I've been tired all day. I have battled sleepiness since after finishing breakfast with our grandparents, and now sleep has won.

# Wheeling and Dealing

## HERCULES LORD

The only reason I haven't shouted, cursing Achilles for being an asshole, is because I don't want to alarm Paisley. As soon as Tabatha, my personal assistant, filed the paperwork for the marriage license, Achilles was somehow alerted. He threatened to change the date on the marriage contract between Lauren and me. I didn't want to do it, but he forced my hand.

After viewing the video of Orion and Lauren, he asked, "Do you really want to destroy our family this way?"

He's waiting for my answer. I stretch my tense neck from side to side. My plan has hit a snag. I wanted to marry Paisley first, just in case her family didn't want to deal. Then they wouldn't be able to take her away from me. She'd be mine. My plan gives us all a happy ending. But Achilles's meddling is screwing it all up.

"I have a plan," I say.

"Hercules, stop fucking around," he roars.

I rub my throbbing temple and remain silent. He needs to calm down. And I know it's going to take him a few beats. I'm certain he's figured out that his best bet is to let me guide the ship.

Achilles hasn't said anything yet, and I take that as a good sign.

"I'm certainly not fucking around here, Achilles. If you file those marriage papers, then I'm sending the video to the trust."

"You'll do that to our family for the fucking Grove girl?"

Anger soars through me. "Paisley. Her name is Paisley."

"What do you want?"

I like his conciliatory tone. "I want to marry Paisley today. Then we need to get Xander and Leo Grove in a room as soon as possible. I have a proposal for them that will solve our problems with the trust from here on out, and it will benefit them too."

Achilles laughs with an edge. "You want to

sneak off and marry Xander's daughter before you try to make a deal with him? I thought you were the smart one."

I squeeze my eyes closed, processing what he just said. Perhaps he's right. Eloping with Xander's daughter is not the best way to ensure trust between our families.

"What is it?" Achilles barks like he's still holding all the cards. Well, he isn't—I am.

"What is what?" I ask curtly.

"What are you proposing?"

I lift my chest and proudly say, "Rules 12.453 and 65.321, together."

Achilles is as silent as a church mouse. I won't speak first, though. I'm certain he knows those rules well. They've always seemed like impossible standards to meet. And granted, our efforts to qualify will be like throwing a Hail Mary pass. But if we succeed, then our family will not only be free from the existing rules of the Lord Trust, but we'll be able to make new rules.

Achilles clears his throat. "Paisley said she'll marry you?"

"Yes." Saying that makes me feel really good. I can hardly believe PG agreed to be my bride. I'm going to love her like no man ever has or ever will.

"Okay," he mutters.

I jerk my head back. "Okay?"

"Yes. Just don't run off to Las Vegas and marry the Grove daughter, you fool. You don't shotgun marry a Grove. Come back to New York. I'll try to set up a meeting today. Stay close to your phone, and I'll let you know when I get it done."

On that note, Achilles and I hang up. As soon as I'm off the line, my cock remembers what it's supposed to be doing right at this exact moment. My chest is knocking. I'm hard, but still, I go to the cockpit and ask Neal and Ross, the pilot and copilot, to see about turning us around and landing at Teterboro instead. The future missus and I won't be going to Las Vegas after all.

---

MY COCK THROBS, AND THE CROTCH OF MY PANTS can hardly contain the size and scale of it when I make it back to the cabin. But Paisley's soft snores rise through the room.

"Shit," I mutter. That took too long. I sensed she'd been tired all morning.

Her bare shoulder is calling my mouth to it, and her breasts aren't covered. I step out of my pants and underwear, and my cock springs forth. I take off my shirt and toss it on the floor. Then my socks and shoes come off before I crawl into bed with her.

Paisley stirs when I press against her. She's warm and soft. So damn soft.

I reach around her curvy hip and press her hard knot.

"Mmm." Touching her feels so good. I rub gently and thoroughly until…

"Mmm," she moans.

"Baby, I need you," I whisper in her ear. "Can I have you?"

She slowly rotates onto her back. Her chin is up. She's sighing heavily because I refuse to stop masturbating her. What a pretty face Paisley has— the angle, the placement of her nose and eyes, her lips. She's the epitome of prettiness. I swallow because I'm trying to keep my excitement in control.

Her back arches as she writhes against my fingers. I roll myself between her legs, and to make her come fast, I go down on her.

I moan. *Oh shit.* Her flavor in my mouth… *Oh shit.* Her high-pitched whimpering and moaning make it hard for me. *Come, baby. Please come.*

Then, having mercy on me, her sex shivers against my mouth, pulsing, and I lap her up. *Damn.*

"Shit," I groan. I'm mad at my cock for taking me to orgasm faster than I wanted to get there.

I don't have much time. I curl my arms around her thighs, lift her ass off the bed, and slam into her hard.

She cries out. Her moans shiver as I pump in and out of her.

*Damn. Damn. Damn. Damn.*

Each thrust takes me closer. Her womanhood is so wet, warm, and tight, grabbing my cock like it loves it.

"Ooh," I say, my voice trembling. I'm at the point of no return.

I spread myself on top of her before I blow. I want to feel Paisley Grove, my future wife, under me—her softness, her femininity. Her air on my neck. Her arms around me, pulling me into her. Then her tongue is against my earlobe.

"Oh shit!" I roar before the most pleasurable sensation a man can feel overtakes me.

I couldn't get enough of PG. But I came so hard that I couldn't get it going again before we landed. She made a deal with me, though. After dealing with her family, we would go back to my place for the night and make love like there was no tomorrow.

I told her that Achilles found out about our plans and threatened to push up the marriage-contract date until I sent him a video. I was never going to tell a soul about the video, but my brother had forced my hand. Then I told her about Lauren and Orion in the hot tub and the plan to make our families allies instead of enemies in complete detail. Paisley listened silently, looking into my eyes with her chin on top of her stacked hands as they rested on my chest.

"No wonder you asked me about Treasure," she said.

"What do you think?"

She snorted an escaped chuckle. "I think she'll never marry Orion. I mean, he was never faithful to her. And then, you captured him on video getting a blow job from your shabby ex-bride-to-be. She'll never allow herself to be tied to him."

I laughed because I'd never heard PG speak so tough about another person. But Lauren deserved the criticism. *Shabby* is the right word for her and Orion.

"But you said Treasure's parents cut her off from her trust fund," I said.

Paisley narrowed an eye cautiously. "Yeah…"

"Maybe this can be a way to collect from your grandfather's trust again."

After puckering her lips and eyebrows thought-fully, PG said, "Maybe. However, I think she does fairly well for herself. I know that she feels if she had the family money that's owed to her, she could stop running herself ragged trying to maintain her extravagant lifestyle."

At first, PG wanted to come with me. She said it would be best if she were in the room to face her father. But I was able to convince her that if her father and uncle turned down our offer, I should drive straight to the airport, and we could continue with our plan to fly to Las Vegas and get married. She liked the sound of that.

Now PG is in bed on my airplane, being waited on by flight personnel until I get back to her. My fingers are crossed. But either way, I'll get the only thing I want in life—my woman.

Greg, who met me at the airport, drops me off in front of the Grove Family Investment Bank building. Leo and Xander were already holding a weekly meeting today at four o'clock, and they agreed that Achilles and I could stop by, and they would give us ten minutes to listen to whatever we had to say.

Achilles said he dangled the Lord Trust's grandfathered bank account in front of them like blood on the nose of a shark. He sounded pretty proud of himself. Achilles can feel it too. It's what I'm feeling —complete and total liberation from the insane rules of the Lord Trust, which have had clans of Lords jumping through hoops to survive and stay wealthy for over a century.

After giving the receptionist my name, the security guard in the lobby escorts me to a private elevator. After I've climbed the distance to the penthouse floor, the elevator opens, and I'm in a large office.

*Damn it. It's already showtime.*

Xander Grove, with his dark hair and glasses, sits in one of four brown leather armchairs. He's made himself comfortable. His brother Leo, who's fairer in hair color and complexion, sits across from him. Achilles is present too. And they're all looking at me.

I lock eyes with Xander Grove. He's going to be

my future father-in-law whether he likes it or not. "Good afternoon, gentlemen," I say.

Frowning bitterly, Leo Grove says, "Your ten minutes start now."

*Ten minutes?* Suddenly, I'm reminded that this is not a gathering of friends. We are still foes.

I start talking before I sit in the only empty chair. This is about money, so I go straight to the money and quote Rules 12.453 and 65.321. "Basically..." I say, scooting to the edge of my seat. "To paraphrase, Lord Trust states that if another 'clan' that is not of Lord kinship offers daughters and a purse that equates to a dowry in the amount five times over the value of the existing trust, then the wealth can be combined and reestablished with the account rules that predate The Bank Holding Act of 1956. That means..."

"I know what it means," Leo says, directing his somber frown at his brother.

Xander Grove's Adam's apple bobs as he swallows.

Achilles and I pass each other a look as the Grove brothers grimace at each other as if they're communicating with their facial expressions. Then my future father-in-law sets his eagle eyes on me. I work like hell not to falter under the force of his stare.

"You're meaning to marry my daughter?"

*Stay strong, Hercules.* "She already said yes." I swallow hard, and they can hear it. Then I sit up straight, shoulders back, legs wide, folding my fingers in front of me. It's a power sit. I need to feel the power right now.

"I love her," I claim. Then, I think about her face, her voice, and all the iterations of Paisley Grove that I've encountered over the years. "I think —no, I know I've loved her for a long time." I can't tell him that I've wanted her ever since I made love to her on that New Year's Eve night over seven years ago. When I woke up in the morning and saw that she was gone, I felt as though I had lost a hand or a foot. Not until last Thursday, when I saw Paisley at Mason and Lake's engagement party, did I know for certain that she was the one—my only one. And this time around, I'll die before I let her family keep her away from me.

Xander Grove's eyes narrow to slits. He's very still, watching me, trying to see through me. I think he thinks I'm bullshitting. Well, I'm not. "Where is she?" he asks.

I want to lie. Gosh, I want to lie. Because he's scaring the hell out of me. "On my airplane."

"What were you planning to do? Run off and marry?" He doesn't sound happy.

*Don't falter, Hercules. Own the truth.* "That was the plan."

Xander Grove looks at Leo and then smirks. Leo chuckles.

"Her mother would've killed you," Xander says. "Tell Paisley we'll let her marry you the right way. Got it?" With his chin dipped and eyebrows raised, he looks at me like he means business.

'That's what I prefer," I say.

Finally, Leo bounds to his feet. "How long do we have?" he asks.

Achilles and I look at each other like we can hardly believe this worked. I stand, and so does my brother.

"The sooner the better," Achilles says. He knows the ball is in their court. That's why my brother can be so effective. He likes to peacock and strut his wings, but he knows when he's been out-feathered. Basically, we're at the Groves' mercy until this deal is finalized. It's up to them to make it happen.

And then we'll be free from our great-grandfather's effective effort to make sure his descendants couldn't plunder his hard-earned wealth. I bet Hugo and Gregory could have never foreseen that one day, our families' relationship could become symbiotic in more ways than one. If this works, Grove Investment Bank will be able to own GIT and LTI. Our company will never have a lack of funds. All Lord descendants will receive yearly payments, equally dispersed from interest earned on the trust and with no stipulations. We shouldn't get any pushback on those terms. But you never know with the Lords.

Regardless, we all look at each other—Achilles at Xander, Xander at Leo, and all of them at me. We know that my marriage to Paisley is a solid bet. But Treasure Grove agreeing to marry one of my brothers—well, that's another story.

# Epilogue

## PAISLEY GROVE

I can't remember which day of the week it is. Not wearing a stitch of clothing, I push the curtains open. Our villa is high on a cliff. Below, sparkling blue waves crash against the stone mountains. We've been to Rome, but Hercules and I prefer the romantic towns along the Amalfi Coast. We arrived in Positano yesterday. And then one hour later, our lives changed forever.

Our families are too occupied by our grandparents' explanation and apology tour to give us much thought. As light filters into our beautiful bedroom, I hold my hand up to the sky to admire my fifty-carat diamond ring. It's so magnificent. I'm generally not into jewelry, but I'm so into this ring my husband has bought me. Hercules and I were married yesterday. It was just the two of us, and our ceremony rocked my world. We couldn't wait for the planned ceremony that our mothers are nitpicking over. We fear something could go wrong between now and the New Year's Eve wedding day. They'll never know we're already married, though. We won't tell them unless we have to.

Hercules had asked me several times whether Treasure would ever agree to marry Orion. And each time, I told him that she would only if she was desperate enough. But I assured him that my cousin was a classic Scorpio who rarely forgave those who crossed her.

And it's because of how difficult it would be to make Treasure say yes to marrying either Lord brother that we decided to get married before the deal could fall apart.

"Admiring the ring again," Hercules says.

I light up as I whip around to face my husband. He's standing in the wide arch of our bedroom, wearing nothing but a towel. I'm hungry for him again. His Adonis-like body is tempting, but it's his face that always steals the show.

"I've never been into jewelry until this," I say, showing him the back of my hand with the ring on it.

He quickly closes the distance between us. I'm in his arms. His body is damp from his swim.

"Mrs. Lord, I need to be inside you." His eyes are full of fire and desire.

Hercules grips two handfuls of my derriere. I'm against him. And he's as hard as steel.

Before our lips can make contact, my cellphone chimes. I've just received a message. We both turn to see whose name is on my screen.

"It's your brother," Hercules says.

I chuckle scoffingly. Max is angry that Leo and my dad made a deal with the Lords without including him. He would've rather used my union with Hercules to leverage me to get TRANSPOT up and running. Then I could have been paid royalties for the new software. That would have put us in the range to receive the Lord Trust account privileges. But the major problem with Max's plan was that it would take years to figure out how to develop TRANSPOT and even longer to make sure it was safe and able to go to market. The Lords can't wait that long. They're on the verge of losing LTI. Well... we're on the verge of losing LTI.

As a reward for packaging the deal with my family, Achilles is allowing Hercules and me to buy LTI. I'm using my Killer Firewall royalties to pay for my half. He's using savings he's accumulated over the years to pay his half.

Hercules raises an eyebrow. "Should we tell him now?"

Surprisingly, seeing Max's name on my screen hasn't quelled my lust. My brother is such a buzzkill. But my sex thumps for the hardness pressing against me.

"No," I whisper before my lips smash against Hercules's.

Then we're on top of our bed.

And then my husband is inside me.

---

*From* **Making It While Faking It (Book 2)**

## TREASURE GROVE - 2 WEEKS LATER

## 6 HOURS LATER

I sit in the back seat of the Grove family chauffeured car, staring into the lobby of the Grove Family Bank Tower past sparkling-clean glass windows. My flight landed in Teterboro less than an hour ago. It felt like forever since I'd flown on a

Grove family private jet. My dad couldn't travel with me. He flew onward to London to handle Grove Industrial Tech, better known as GIT, business. I'm relieved that we parted ways. I wouldn't know what to say to him during a five-hour flight to New York City. But I am back in a big way. Everything around me is Grove, Grove, Grove. Soon, my bank account will reflect that I too am a thorough Grove yet again, and I will no longer be a cutoff heiress with serious cash-flow problems.

On the flight over the Atlantic Ocean, I constantly worried about the deal we brokered going south before the wheels of the airplane touched ground. But I made it to my final destination, and as far as I'm aware, the deal is still on. I can already feel the money gracing my fingertips.

The driver opens my door, and when I have two feet on the sidewalk, he says, "I'll be waiting for you, Miss Grove."

Before I can say there's no need to wait, my attention is hijacked by a tall, strapping man wearing an impeccable suit. For some reason, I can't look away from him. His gait resembles that of someone who descends from royalty. And it's not his neatly trimmed five-o'clock shadow, perfectly formed forehead, sharp cheekbones, and kissable lips that steal my attention either—it's his confidence that demands to be noticed.

As if sensing me staring, the man stops and turns. I suspend breathing when our eyes meet. His face looks... oh my God. I gasp a quick breath of air. It's him—my new fake fiancé and soon to be husband.

---

## 6 HOURS AGO

That was brutal.

The pressure in my head builds toward explosion as I flee the live set where an actual TV show is being filmed. Several of my emotions battle each other for the top spot. I'm embarrassed, angry, fed up with this whole ordeal, and plain old sad. Pinching the bridge of my nose, I force the tears that want to come gushing from my eyes to stay put. I refuse to give Liam Caruso, our jerk director, the satisfaction of knowing he made me cry. He's been on a mission to break me ever since day one, and maybe he finally has. It's too soon to tell.

The morning air is chilly, but storming off the set generated a lot of body heat, so I'm too hot to feel the cold. I'm walking so fast that I'm practically running. I glance over my shoulder. The makeshift wooden wall built around a dirt pit that's supposed to be the inside of medieval manor is in the distance. Finally, I'm far enough from the scene of the crime to slow my pace and catch my breath.

"The horses are famished, Father—are you certain they can take the journey?" I whisper in the accented voice of my character.

I have such a horrible English accent. And damn it—it's "make the journey," not "take the journey."

I stop at the edge of a wooden floor built between two long rows of star trailers and lift my face to the opaque gray overcast. My eyes flicker closed as I groan in misery. In my head, I hear my dad's voice asking if I'm ready to take any responsibility for Caruso blowing up and kicking me off the set.

"Okay," I whisper against a refreshingly mild wind. I messed up my lines.

Before botching "make," I said "Mother" instead of "Father." And before that, I said "hamished," which isn't even a real word, instead of "famished." Sigh... My head and heart just isn't in this whole acting thing.

**From Z.L. Arkadie, writing as Zoey Locke comes a brand new contemporary billionaire romance about two people who are total opposites accepting a marriage pact to get themselves out of desperate situations. *Making It While Faking It*, a passionate standalone and swoony page-turner, is book two of The Lords of Manhattan series.**

A new pair of singles from the Lord and Grove families are engaged.

They should be able to keep it strictly business since she's the life of the party and he doesn't like people-- right? They're the sort of the opposites that will never attract.

Plus, they don't actually have to live together.

For five years their marriage will be on paper only. However, they can't screw this up. If the world finds out they're faking, then it will all be for naught.

Everything goes as planned until two exes ruin everything.

Now, these total opposites find themselves asking yet again...

They should not be feeling butterflies or any kind of yearning feelings for each other, right?

In theory, two people like them should never be attracted to each other, right?

Wrong.

Continue with the Lords and Groves in *Making It Will Faking It*, **Lords of Manhattan** (Book 2).

**Get Your Copy!**

## MINGLING OF LORDS AND GROVES

*❝ Breaking news!*

*Sources say it's official. Pop the champagne and blast the streamers. The new money heiress, Paisley Grove, and the old money billionaire, Hercules Lord have made it official. We're not talking engagement people. During a whirlwind romantic getaway, the couple stole away to the Amalfi coast, and in a majestic little seacoast town called Positano, they tied the knot.*

*Paisley Rose Grove is now officially Paisley Rose Lord.*

*Or not.*

*The couple denies they're married.*

*But we know better.*

*We have proof. But for legal purposes, we are not allowed to publish our receipts--yet.*

*Regardless of what they want to call themselves, we at Top Rag Mag are sending them well wishes and good luck. Their brothers still hate each other.*

*However, the heiress is winning, and the distant cousin is losing.*

*By the way, did you check out last week's post of the distant cousin threatening the heiress like a petty stick-up woman on the mean streets of New York? It means nothing now that the heiress has the man, but check out the video below because it's juicy.*

*We can drop the mic on this post as it stands, but there's more!*

*Are you ready for this?*

*Sources say that our beloved Treasure Grove is also hooked-up with a Lord brother. They're engaged. But we don't know to which of the hunky billionaires--the beast or the playboy.*

*Stay tuned--this juicy story is still developing.*

Sure he's a billionaire. Sure he's tall, dark, and handsome to the extreme. But he's more so crabby, frigid, and a regular storm cloud. And yes, he's my new fake fiancé. But when opposites start to attract, could we end up making it while it?

*Making It While Faking It*
**BUY IT TODAY!**